Albert and the Witches of Harborville

By J. S. Schaya

Cover Art by Kaley and Lauren Phillips

ISBN: 153087128X
ISBN 13: 9781530871285

Library of Congress Control Number:
2016919696
CreateSpace Independent Publishing
Platform, North Charleston, SC

For my grandchildren, present and future.
And for my husband and sons, you are my
always and forever.

Prologue

A Pairing

"Well, I guess I'm going to have to come up with a name for you," said Catrina Cantwick, as she petted the orange-and-white tabby cat sitting next to her in the car. "Hmmm, what to name an orange cat caught on All Hallow's Eve.

"If you hadn't trapped me, you wouldn't have to worry about it," replied the tabby.

Catrina kept right on driving as if talking cats were as everyday an occurrence as the sun rising each morning.

"It was either trap you or watch you starve, and we couldn't have that, now, could we?" said Catrina.

Did I happen to mention that Catrina Cantwick is a witch? Not that you'd ever know by looking at her. You see, there's a misconception about witches. Most believe they are ugly, old hags with black, stringy hair and warts on their noses, but this couldn't be any further from the truth. Witches look just like mortals. Stand a witch and a mortal side by side, and unless you're a witch yourself, you'd never know the difference. And this business about them living on the dark side of the moon and riding broomsticks—pure rubbish! They live in cities and towns just like everyone else and, for some reason that can't quite be explained, tend to drive Volkswagens. You should also know that they rise each morning; read the daily newspaper; drink coffee, tea, or orange juice with their breakfast; then get on with their day just like ordinary people. The only difference is that they possess a special kind of magic that isn't found in your everyday mortal.

Oh, one other thing you should know about witches—they are not mean and evil. Sure, there are a few out there who give the others a bad name, but for the most part, witches are kind, sweet, caring individuals who would as soon swallow a bullfrog as commit a mean act or hurt someone's feelings. The world could definitely use a few more witches.

Well, now that we've gotten all that out of the way, sit back and make yourself comfortable, because I'm about to tell you the story of how three cats, two librarians, and one extraordinarily gifted field mouse named Albert saved an entire town from—well, you'll see.

It all started one spring morning when the Harborville Town Council decided to tear down an old, abandoned caretaker's cottage to make room for a parking lot. The town council members thought the additional parking would be a great convenience for the residents of their town. They failed, however, to take into consideration what a very big inconvenience it would be for one orange-and-white tabby cat that had made her home in the cottage's loft or for all the field mice that dwelled in the meadow grass that surrounded it.

Anyway, in late September the cottage came down, leaving the cat homeless, and a few days later large trucks came, graded the field, and poured a thick layer of hot, black tar that left the mice running for the hills. Well, actually, in this case they went running for the window of the public library where they set up housekeeping in the basement. The poor cat, however, was forced to find shelter elsewhere. It was the night she found herself lying in the Havermans' damp doghouse that she realized she had hit rock bottom and began to entertain thoughts of living with Catrina Cantwick, a local witch who worked for the library. After all, to live the life of a witch's cat meant to live a life of comfort. Coincidentally, Catrina had been thinking how nice it would be to share her home with a certain orange-and-white tabby that had taken to hanging around the back stairs of the library where she worked.

Now, there is a big difference between the relationship an ordinary mortal has with a cat and that which develops between a witch and a cat. For starters, mortals cannot carry on conversations with their cats and tend to keep them as pets. Witches, on the other hand, spend much of their time discussing matters of great intellectual importance with their feline friends and consider them compassionate companions. Did I mention that witches are able to converse with all animals? Well, they can. As a matter of fact, a witch can carry on a conversation just as easily with an aardvark as an attorney, only she'd probably prefer chatting with the aardvark— witches are extremely good judges of character.

Another difference is that when mortals want a cat, they usually look in the paper under "Giveaways" or visit a pet store, where they are presented with a variety of choices. They then choose the cat that looks the best to them and take it home. The cat rarely, if ever, has any say in the matter. This is not at all how witches and cats pair up. You see, there are rules that must be followed in order for a cat and a witch to share a home. First, only witches who are twelve years and older and have developed a sense of whimsy may pair with a cat; second, the witch who desires the cat must trap it without the use of witchcraft on All Hallow's Eve (Halloween, for all you mortals out there); and third, the cat must want to belong to the witch who is doing the trapping. These are very strict rules that date back centuries.

So on October 31st, Catrina parked her yellow Volkswagen Beetle next to the orange tabby, which appeared to be waiting for her on the corner of First and Main, and opened the door on the passenger side. The tabby nodded politely and jumped in. Catrina then shut the door, thereby trapping the cat securely in her car. Now, obviously, the cat knew exactly what was going on, or it would never have come near a car that smelled of witch— a kind of cross between lavender and jasmine.

"So," said Catrina, reaching over and giving the cat's ear a gentle tug, "you were caught on All Hallow's

Eve. How about we call you Eve? That is, unless you have something else in mind."

"Eve," purred the cat. "I like it."

"Great, then Eve it is." Thus began the friendship between Catrina and Eve.

1

Albert

The Harborville Town Library stood at the corner of Main and Dunlap Streets. It was a warm, cozy, two-story building whose entire first floor was dedicated to the children's library. There were kid-size tables with kid-size chairs and bookshelves that were placed at just the right height for those who had not as yet been afflicted with tallness. The windows along the back wall were framed with bright-colored curtains, and the far left corner was home to a rocking chair and soft rug where one could stretch out in the sun and enjoy a good story. But what caught everyone's eye as they entered was the ceiling, for suspended from its center, wings spread as if in flight, was a four-and-a-half-foot-long soft sculpture of Mother Goose, complete with bonnet and bifocals.

Catrina, along with two other librarians, Annie Arkinson and Wanda Schwartz, made up the staff of the children's library. Annie was a young, tall, dark-haired witch whose energetic approach to life came in quite handy on Tuesday afternoons when the library played host to the town's preschool program, and Wanda was a plump, kind, middle-aged woman who, though mortal, possessed her own particular kind of magic. You see, it was absolutely impossible to spend more than two minutes with Wanda and not walk away with that contented feeling one gets when eating warm cookies straight from the oven.

It was Wanda who had looked the other way when, in late September, mice began showing up in the library's basement. Eventually, she confided in Catrina and Annie about their arrival, but only because she was caught sneaking down the basement stairs with a bag full of mouse treats from Crates of Critters, Harborville's only pet store. The three agreed the mice presence should be kept a secret. After all, it wouldn't do to have Miss Prattle find out about them.

Miss Prattle was the Director of Services for the Harborville Town Library, though how she had gotten the job, no one knew. She was a thin, strict-looking woman with an angular chin, beady eyes, and a pointed nose. Her short, black hair was cut in a V-shaped pageboy and framed a face that was accustomed to wearing a scowl. In the six months that she had been the library's director, she had made it quite clear that she didn't like dogs, cats, or kids. As a matter of fact, Miss Prattle didn't appear to like much of anything except for an odd-looking plant she kept under a special grow light in a corner of her office. Fortunately, the rest of the staff rarely had to deal with her, as she seldom strayed from her office on the second floor.

It was shortly after the mass migration of mice into the library's basement that Catrina and Annie called a meeting of the new residents.

"Is everyone present?" implored Catrina, tucking her short, blond hair behind her ears. "Can everyone hear me?"

There were multiple squeaks from all directions as the mice settled down and stared intently at Catrina and Annie.

"We understand your dilemma," stated Catrina, squinting into the far corners of the room, "and Annie and I want you to know that you're welcome to stay as long as you like. However, we are going to have to establish a few ground rules." This last statement was met by a few groans from some of the adolescent mice, who had gathered on the ledge of the furnace.

"To start with," said Annie, stepping forward, "we can't have any of the books or magazines in the library damaged in any way. That means no tearing them up for nests, fun, or anything else you might have in mind. As a matter of fact, let's just say that they are totally off limits." She looked directly at the group perched on the furnace ledge. "Also, you absolutely cannot make your presence known to anyone other than Catrina and myself. Not all mortals are fond of furry things, and if they become aware that you are living down here, it could present a problem for all of us. So please, do not go above the basement level unless the library is completely void of mortals, with the exception of Wanda, of course. Also, please bear in mind that Wanda is a mortal and cannot communicate with any of you, nor is she aware that Catrina and I are witches. So if you have any questions, please direct them to either Cat or myself. Now, if I could please call your attention to the wall, I'll explain the transit system to you." Annie pointed to various places along the wall and began making circular motions with her index finger. As she did, small portals appeared, each bearing the picture of a local landmark.

"Now, since we can't have you running in and out of the windows at all hours," said Annie motioning toward the wall, "we request that you use these designated tunnels to enter and leave the basement. Each tunnel is clearly marked and leads to a different location in town. The cup and saucer represents the Earthly Brew Coffee House, the house represents Merris Merriweather's real estate office, and so on and so forth. All of these businesses are witch owned, and their proprietors have agreed to aid in your comings and goings. A spell has been cast on each opening that makes it invisible to mortals, so please do not use an exit when Wanda is around, as we're not sure how she would react to disappearing mice."

"Well, that about covers it," said Catrina. "Are there any questions? Yes, you in the back." Catrina acknowledged a young, studious-looking mouse that was perched on top of a cigar box along with his parents and eleven brothers and sisters. "Name, please?"

"Albert," squeaked the mouse.

"And your question, Albert?"

11

"Do you leave any lights on in the library at night?" At this, Albert's eleven brothers and sisters burst out laughing.

"Albert's afraid of the dark!" they chortled. "Albert's afraid of the dark!"

"I am not!" shot back Albert.

"Calm down, all of you, right now!" warned their mother, giving them a stern look.

Catrina waited as Albert's siblings composed themselves.

"It has always been our policy to keep a small lamp on next to the rocking chair in the story corner," she assured Albert. "Any other questions? No? Well, then, we'll be leaving now," said Catrina, as she and Annie gathered up their coats and purses. "See you all tomorrow. I'm sure we'll all get along famously as long as everyone follows the rules."

Albert was quiet for the rest of the evening. He waited patiently until his eleven brothers and sisters were asleep for the night, then quietly made his way up the stairs and into the children's library. His mother saw him go but gave no indication that she was aware of him leaving. Nor did she say anything three hours later, as Albert tiptoed past his sleeping siblings and crawled back into bed.

The next morning, when Wanda opened the library, she noticed a book lying open on the soft rug in the children's corner.

Odd, thought Wanda. *Wonder who left this here?*

2

Caught

"Cat, do you have any idea how this got here?" inquired Annie, retrieving a book from the floor next to the rocking chair.

"I don't know. A ghost?" offered up Catrina, raising an eyebrow.

"Or mouse," speculated Annie. "Remember that little guy who wanted to know if we left a light on at night?"

"Right, Albert." Catrina smiled. "You don't suppose he can read, do you?"

"I don't know, but Wanda said she's found a book lying open on the floor in the story corner every morning for the last week." The two witches exchanged glances.

"It could be one of the mice," said Catrina. "Then again, it might be something a little more difficult to deal with. Remember last year when that banshee decided to roost in the barn of one of Merris's rental properties?"

"Who can forget?" replied Annie. "Not only did the witch's council have to come up with a plausible story to explain all the wailing, but it took Merris two months to convince her to relocate. Said she had made a pet of a turkey vulture that lived nearby and didn't want to leave him. Boy, was she a work of art."

The two decided to stick around that night on the chance their nightly guest would pay another visit.

Catrina had brought Eve with her, as was usually the case on Fridays, and after the library closed, the three enjoyed a picnic on the floor.

After dinner Catrina and Annie pulled chairs up next to the window, where they read the *Witch's Weekly News* by moonlight, and Eve went off to explore small, dark spaces among the stacks. She was just getting ready to attack a particle only a cat could see when she caught a glimpse of something scurrying along the edge of the carpet. Her eyes narrowed and she crouched, waiting for it to move again. When it did, she pounced, capturing it between her front paws. At that moment the lights came on and Eve found herself staring down at a small, brown mouse.

"Please don't eat me!" squeaked a terrified Albert.

"As if any self-respecting, well-fed cat would eat the likes of you," replied Eve.

Albert couldn't help but to feel both relieved and insulted.

"You would make an interesting toy, though," purred Eve, giving him a light bat with her paw.

Albert tried to run, but he hadn't made it more than two feet before a large, orange paw came down on his tail, pinning him to the rug.

Catrina walked over to Eve and stared down at the small mouse. "Albert, is that you?"

"Yes, ma'am," said Albert, heart racing. He knew he wasn't supposed to be near the books, but he just couldn't help himself, and now he was caught. He knew he deserved whatever punishment he was about to receive and was trying hard to take it like a mouse, but his whiskers were quivering, and he was shaking so badly he could hardly stand.

"For goodness sake, calm down," said Catrina. "No one's going to hurt you. We just want to ask you a few questions with regard to some books."

At this Albert launched into a confession.

"I know I wasn't supposed to touch them," wailed Albert, "but I didn't hurt them, honest, I didn't. I have a great deal of respect for books. I would never harm one. And I would have put them back, really I would have, but I'm not strong enough to get them back on the shelves. It took everything I had just to push them off and drag them over here to the light."

Catrina and Annie watched as Albert, breathless from his speech, fell to his knees and began to beg for mercy.

"Please don't make me leave," pleaded Albert. "There's no place on this whole earth I'd rather live than in this library. Please let me stay."

"Dramatic little thing, isn't he?" said Annie, who was trying not to laugh.

"No one's asking you to leave," soothed Catrina, who was hardly able to suppress her own giggles.

"You mean you're not throwing me out?" asked Albert hopefully.

"Of course not," answered Catrina. "What would give you that idea?"

"I touched the books," said Albert, hanging his head. "You allowed us to stay, and all you asked was that we not touch the books, and I broke the rules, but I just couldn't help myself."

"Albert," said Catrina, reaching down and removing Eve's paw from his tail. "Can you read?"

"Yes. Yes, I can," replied Albert proudly.

Catrina and Annie stared at each other. A reading mouse was an oddity, even for them.

"Who taught you?" asked Annie.

"I taught myself," said Albert, his voice full of pride. "My father used to bring home paper from the trash can outside the elementary school. You know, the kind with the lines that kids practice their ABCs on. Anyway, Mom said it made the best nesting material, and she used to line our beds with it. But I liked studying it better than sleeping on it, and before long, I could read the whole alphabet. Then I graduated to the pieces of newspaper Dad brought home to me from the recycling bin outside the dump. But this is the first time," said Albert, his voice filling with emotion, "that I've had the opportunity to read books. This has been the best week of my life." Albert sat on the rug and tried to hold back a tear. "I didn't mean to hurt anything," he sniffed, "and I promise I won't touch them again."

"Don't be silly," said Annie, reaching down and scooping Albert into her hand. She placed him on the seat of the rocking chair. "You're welcome to read all the books you like."

"Really?" squeaked Albert. He could hardly believe what he was hearing. Instead of being asked to leave, he was being told he could read to his heart's content.

"Don't look so surprised," said Catrina. "After all, we are librarians. We promote literacy, even in mice. However, I do think we need to come up with a better way for you to handle your reading material. Let's try this."

Catrina removed a pair of black bifocals from a chain around her neck, laid them in front of Albert, waved her hand over them, and chanted, "Tiny as a mere book louse, reduce these spectacles for a mouse." The glasses began to tremble and make a high, shrill whistling noise. Then, right before Albert's eyes, they shrank until they were a perfect fit for him.

"Well, don't just sit there," said Annie impatiently. "Try them on."

Albert picked up the glasses and placed them on his nose.

"How do they feel?" asked Catrina.

"Fine," answered Albert trying not to sound ungrateful, "but I don't need glasses. I can see just fine."

"Oh, they're not for reading," said Catrina. "They're for shrinking."

"Shrinking," gasped Albert. "How small do you want me to get?" Perhaps he was to be punished after all.

"Don't be silly," said Annie. "They're not for shrinking you. They're for shrinking books."

"Let's try them out, shall we?" said Catrina. She lifted Albert up and placed him on a bookshelf.

"Now," said Catrina, "I want you to browse around until you find a book that interests you, then I want you to stare at it as hard as you possibly can, and try not to blink."

Albert set about following his instructions. He chose a volume of children's verse and stared intently at its cover. At first nothing happened, then just as he was about to ask the point of the exercise, the book began to shake. It made a shrill, whistling noise and shrank until it was the perfect size for a mouse.

"That's the ticket," cheered Annie.

"Well done," said Catrina.

Albert couldn't believe his eyes. Sitting in front of him, just the right size for him to hold and read, was the book.

"All right, Albert," said Catrina, picking up the mouse and placing him on the palm of her hand. "Now that we've got things down to your size, so to speak, we'll be expecting you every evening at closing. You're to wait until the last patron leaves, then you can browse the shelves and make your selections before we turn out the overhead lights. When you're ready to leave, place any books you have finished under the cushion of the rocking chair, and Annie and I will return them to their proper size and place them back on the shelves when we come in to work."

"Catrina," said Albert, concern in his voice, "don't *you* need your glasses?"

"Heavens, no!" said Catrina. "I just wore them because little Sue Ellen Whittaker thought they made me look more librarian-like, and she moved away two months ago, so they'll never be missed."

"I don't know how to thank you," said Albert. "You've made me the happiest mouse in the world."

3

A Problem with Prattle

In the weeks that followed, things went along smoothly. Miss Prattle remained locked up in her office on the second floor, where she continued to fuss over her strange plant; Catrina and Annie volunteered to close nights, enabling Albert to browse the shelves each evening; and Wanda, who was a morning person, got to open and leave early. There was only one tricky moment when one of Albert's cousins slipped up and used a tunnel while Wanda was in the basement celebrating her new hours by passing out mouse treats from her Crates of Critters bag. Fortunately for all concerned, Wanda attributed the disappearing mouse to needing her glasses changed, as any alternate explanation would have required a visit to Dr. Myers, the local psychiatrist. Albert felt badly about the incident, but when Wanda showed up at work the following morning sporting a new pair of designer frames and feeling quite good about herself, his conscience was eased.

Eve became a more frequent visitor to the library, and after a shaky start, she and Albert became friends. They even invented their own game, which they playfully referred to as *cat and mouse*. It was a kind of hide and seek game, in which Eve would stalk Albert and practice her pouncing. Albert would use his best mouse diversion tactics to avoid being caught, but in the end, Eve would always manage to corner him—usually under the circulation desk—pounce, and then proceed to tickle him with her sandpaper tongue until the small mouse doubled over with laughter.

Perhaps it was because things were going along so well, or perhaps it was because Miss Prattle never seemed to stray from her office, but after a while Catrina and Annie, who rarely if ever had to deal with the starch-faced woman, just sort of forgot about her. At least they did until one Friday night in mid-May.

You see, Miss Prattle had always made it a point to stay out of the children's library, so it came as quite a surprise to all concerned when she announced her presence at the door one evening by giving out a loud shriek.

"What is that filthy rat doing in here?" she screamed. She raised her black-handled umbrella executioner's style over her head.

The timing could not have been worse. Catrina and Annie, who were straightening the lower bookshelves, were taken completely off guard and Albert, who was right in the middle of a fast game of *cat and mouse* with Eve, was caught out in the open while on his way to the book bin.

"I'll get you, you rodent!" hissed Miss Prattle, coming down hard on the floor with her umbrella handle.

Albert, who was standing wide-eyed and stunned in the middle of the floor, barely had time to move before the black enameled handle came crashing down, striking his left ear just hard enough to send him rolling onto his back. He looked up, heart racing, as Miss Prattle prepared to deliver another blow. At that moment Albert, who had just given up all hope of ever reading another book, heard a low growl come from behind the stacks, followed by an explosion of hissing. Everyone turned just in time to see a furious Eve bound across the floor, scoop a startled Albert into her mouth, and jump out an open window.

"How many of those awful vermin have you seen?" demanded Miss Prattle, her black beady eyes peering over her pointed nose. "There's never just one you know. If there's one, there's a hundred. I'm calling the exterminator first thing next week. They'll deal with those ugly, disease-ridden pests. And Catrina," she said, turning toward the door, "if you insist on bringing that cat in here, make sure it gets a flea treatment and have it checked for mange." She turned back around. "I almost forgot, everyone upstairs in the adult library will be attending a conference over the weekend, and I'm expecting some packages. I've arranged to have them left in the book drop. Tell Wanda when she empties the book drop to place the packages outside my office door." She then turned on her heel and left without so much as a goodbye.

"Have me checked for mange, indeed," sputtered an indignant Eve, after spitting a bewildered Albert onto the soft rug in the children's corner. "She's the one who should be checked for mange, along with any other disgusting parasites silly enough to call her home!" Eve looked down at a slightly soggy Albert and placed a dry paw gently on his head. "Albert, are you all right?" She didn't hurt your ear too badly, I hope."

Albert raised a shaky paw and felt for the lump he knew would be gracing the back of his ear. "No," he said bravely, "she just nicked me. Thank you, Eve. If it hadn't been for you, I would have been a goner."

"Think nothing of it," purred Eve. "I'm just sorry I didn't get to you sooner."

Albert looked up and saw Annie and Catrina staring at each other. The two appeared to be deeply concerned about something.

"What's the matter?" questioned Albert. "If it's me you're worried about, there's no need. I'm fine."

"We're glad you're all right, Albert," said Annie, "but it's Miss Prattle who has us concerned. She's calling an exterminator."

Albert froze. An exterminator was a mouse's worst nightmare, for if there was one about, a mouse didn't stand a chance.

"What are we going to do?" squeaked Albert, trying not to tremble.

"Evacuate all mice," sighed Catrina. "There's no other choice."

"But where will we go?" cried Albert.

Catrina picked Albert up and held him in the palm of her hand. "Don't worry, Albert," she said soothingly. "The witch's council is meeting at the Earthly Brew tomorrow night. We'll put our heads together and come up with a plan. In the meantime, I don't want you to mention this to anyone. It could create a panic."

Albert tried to put on a brave front, but underneath he was quite shaken.

"I'm a little tired," he said, clutching his tail between his paws. "If it's all right with you, I think I'll go downstairs to bed."

"Good idea," said Catrina, placing the exhausted little mouse on the floor. "You've had a trying night. You should get some rest."

Albert slumped over to the children's corner, picked up his glasses from where he'd left them on the rug, and gently placed them into the hem of the curtains where he kept them for safekeeping. He then crept wearily toward the stairs, feeling as though he was carrying the weight of the world on his small shoulders. *How could I have been so careless as not to watch for Prattle?* he thought to himself glumly. *I've ruined everything.*

4

The Earthly Brew

The Earthly Brew Coffeehouse stood halfway down Main Street, seven blocks east of the library and eight blocks west of the elementary school. At 11:00 p.m. on the second Saturday of each month, the blinds that covered the establishment's glass front windows were drawn tight to block the view from the street, and the parking lot that stood adjacent to its back door filled with Volkswagens that smelled of jasmine and lavender. This was because the coffeehouse' owners, Basil and Helen Bramblewood, hosted the regular monthly meetings of the local witch's council.

The Bramblewoods, a most loving and respected witch couple, were the proud parents of two children: Braden Evan, a sturdy, good-natured boy of fourteen and Bailey Cassle, a bright, energetic, green-eyed girl of exactly eleven and three-quarters, if you wanted to be precise, and Bailey did.

"Three months from today, I'll be twelve," stated Bailey happily, as she helped her brother push the wooden tables that represented a variety of shapes and sizes to the side of the room. "You know what that means!"

"That on Halloween you'll finally be old enough to trap yourself a cat. If you can find one that'll have you," teased Braden. He noticed a look of concern spread across his sister's face and quickly added, "Just kidding. I'm sure there are dozens of cats out there that would be honored to pair up with you. Right, Sebastian?"

"Absolutely," purred the black and white tomcat sitting on the windowsill. "If a scraggly sort like your brother can attract a well-marked cat such as myself, just imagine what's coming your way."

"Very funny," replied Braden.

Bailey gave one last table a shove and began lining the chairs up in rows. Beside each chair she placed a broom, brush side up. When she was done, she stood in front of the chairs and asked the brooms to "please rise," which they did, approximately four inches off the floor. And not a minute too soon, as the witches, accompanied by their cats, began arriving.

Catrina and Annie were among the first to arrive, accompanied by Eve and Annie's calico cat, Paisley.

"Basil, Helen, so nice to see you. The place looks great as always!" remarked Cat, as she walked through the door. "And I'll bet the plants were your idea," she said, winking at Bailey and pointing to the catnip bushes that kept springing up at random around the room.

"Come Halloween, I'll have a barn full of kittens," remarked Merris Merriweather wistfully, patting Bailey on the head as she passed by. "That is, if anyone's interested." She smiled at Helen and Basil. "Braden, I swear you've grown an inch since Thursday. Come, sit, and tell me how school's going. Is Andrew still helping Miss Johnson get the elementary school kids safely across the street in the mornings?"

Andrew was the McFarlands' Border collie. The McFarlands, who were getting on in age, had recently sold their sheep farm and moved into town, leaving Andrew with nothing to herd, or so they thought until they caught him one morning, making certain all the children stayed within the crosswalk in front of the elementary school—a job that earned him not only a hug from the crossing guard each morning but also recognition from the mayor in the form of a Good Citizen Award presented at the Founders' Day celebration.

"Yeah, he's still crossing kids. He hasn't missed a day since the school year started. He should be around here some place. We're keeping an eye on him while the McFarlands are away at her sister's. As we speak," said Braden, watching as a black and white collie entered the room, nudging a small Persian kitten along in front of him.

"Lucy, I believe this belongs to you," said the collie. He gently picked the kitten up with his mouth and placed it in Lucy Liggenlathen's lap. "He almost got himself locked in the back cupboard."

"Herman, what am I going to do with you?" scolded the gray-haired witch, as she picked up the kitten and placed it on her shoulder. "Thank you, Andrew. I don't know what we'd do without you."

"Think nothing of it," sighed the collie. "Glad to be of service."

"Hello Andrew," called Merris, waving from her seat in the middle row. "Are the kids staying inside the crosswalk for you in the mornings?"

"Yes," answered Andrew. "All except for the Goodman's youngest, Ellie. She's all over the place, but she's only five, and I'm sure with a little more training, she'll catch on."

The truth was that Ellie knew she was supposed to stay within the lines of the crosswalk, but she loved Andrew so much that she stepped out on purpose just to get his attention.

It was almost eleven and time for the meeting to begin.

"Could everyone take their seats, please?" requested Carl Cunningham, a short, thin witch whose bulbous nose boasted a pair of eyeglasses so large they resembled a windshield.

There was a bit of confusion as the witches accounted for their cats and settled into their chairs.

"I'd like to open by thanking the Bramblewoods for hosting our meetings," said Carl, motioning for the Bramblewoods to stand. "I don't know what we'd do without them." There were murmurs of thanks as the Bramblewoods rose, nodded politely at their guests, and then took their seats.

"Now let's see what's on the agenda for tonight. Oh, yes, the 2,303rd annual Witchfest has been scheduled for August 22nd. It's going to be held in the Dark Caverns of Hanhoo, below the Black Hills. The reservations committee would like to get an idea of how many rooms to book, so if you plan on attending, would you please raise your broom?"

Seven of the brooms that were hovering four inches off the floor shot up another eight.

"Let me see now, that's five, six, seven," said Carl counting the brooms hanging in the air. "I think twelve rooms should be enough. Remember, if you're interested in going, deposits have to be in by June 1st."

The rest of the meeting moved along as usual. There was a report of a haunting at the Yarlsbough Inn, but as the mortal couple who owned the establishment was overheard saying that they felt the ghost was good for business, it was decided that the entity should not be asked to leave.

It was reported that Merris's niece, Candace, had used one of the spells published in the *Witch's Weekly News* to water the plants in her parlor, and when she got to the part that read "rain cats and dogs," four Siamese and a Beagle trickled down before she could call a halt to it. Needless to say, there was unanimous assent that future spells be tried out by the editor prior to publication.

Members were reminded that witches only made up a small portion of Harborville's population, and parents were asked to remind their children not to perform magic in public. Apparently, the previous Monday, a well-meaning six-year-old girl stopped the rain over the only person standing at the bus stop without an umbrella, and the unusual weather pattern had created quite a stir among the mortal population.

The cats took a moment to thank Bailey for the catnip bushes—at least those that weren't too busy chasing the bushes took a moment to thank Bailey for the catnip bushes—and it was announced that by Halloween a certain young lady might just be in the market to trap a cat.

Carl called for old business and received no response. He then called for new business, and Catrina's broom rose high into the air.

"Yes, Catrina," Carl smiled. "What can we do for you?"

"Actually, it's what you can do for the library mice," said Catrina. "You see, we're having a bit of a problem with Miss Prattle." Catrina could not help but notice that foreheads furrowed and noses wrinkled at the mere mention of the woman's name.

"What's that strict, sour face done now?" questioned Lucy, pulling Herman off the back of the chair in front of her.

"She found Albert," replied Catrina, watching as Herman crawled up his mistress's sleeve and made his way down the back of Lucy's neck, "and she's calling an exterminator. I'm afraid we're going to have to evacuate the mice. If any of you could be so kind as to house a family or two, would you please raise a broom?"

Every broom rose a full foot off the floor.

"I've got three empty barns on the edge of town," volunteered Merris Merriweather. "And we can extend the tunnel system from the real estate office to the farms."

"I can always use a few extra paws around the store," said Bianca Beechwood, a young, intelligent witch with long, auburn hair and brown eyes. Bianca owned the health food store at the end of Main Street and was the best herbalist the witch's council had ever had the pleasure of knowing.

"Let's all work out an evacuation plan over refreshments," suggested Helen Bramblewood, pulling cups that resembled small black caldrons with half-moons on them out of a cabinet and placing them on saucers.

"Excellent idea," commented Carl Cunningham, calling the meeting to a close and helping himself to a freshly brewed caldron of coffee.

Plans were made for the evacuation, and witches and cats were making their way out the door, when Basil stopped Catrina in the hallway.

"Catrina," he said, "I need to talk to you about a delivery that was made to the library."

"A delivery?" questioned Cat.

"Yes, shortly before the meeting, I saw a man in a dark coat place several packages in the library's book drop at the back steps. The objects didn't appear to be books, so I thought I should mention it to you."

"Well, Miss Prattle did say she was expecting some deliveries over the weekend," said Catrina, "but it is odd that they would come so late. Thanks for letting us know, Basil. We'll check with Wanda about it on Monday."

5

Parting Plans

"Why, that—! How dare she? Well, I ought to—" exclaimed Wanda, as Cat and Annie told her about Miss Prattle's plan to exterminate the building.

"Calm down, Wanda," said Cat, staring wide-eyed at her friend. She had never seen Wanda so upset.

"Calm down! Calm down! How am I supposed to calm down when that beady-eyed, little biddy is planning to murder our mice!" This was the first time that either Cat or Annie had heard Wanda utter a disparaging word against anyone.

"Those poor little creatures," continued Wanda, "have never done a thing to merit someone calling an exterminator on them. In the entire time they have been here, they have never gnawed on a single book or so much as torn into one magazine. They're not doing any harm. Why can't she just leave them alone?" Wanda stomped toward the door. "The nerve of that woman. First she tried to cut back the hours for the summer reading program, then she complained the preschoolers were making too much noise, and now this. Well, I for one have had enough. I think it's high time Miss Prattle and I had a little talk."

"Wanda," said Annie, who was absolutely astonished by Wanda's gumption. "I don't think talking to Miss Prattle is going to help the situation. Besides, she's not here. She's still attending the conference. But you needn't worry. We're not going to let the exterminators harm the mice. We've got a plan."

"What kind of a plan?" asked Wanda, raising an eyebrow.

"We're simply going to run all the mice out of the basement prior to the exterminator's arrival, then we'll lock the windows up tight so they can't get back in. The weather is warm now, so they should be fine."

Wanda looked doubtful, but as she could not think of a better solution, she agreed that it would be the best approach.

"The problem," said Wanda, looking forlorn, "is that they're going to think we don't like them or want them here, and nothing could be further from the truth."

Cat and Annie knew that over the past months Wanda had begun to think of the mice as pets, but it was not until now that they realized the extent of her attachment. It was going to be hard for Wanda to evict the mice, even if it was for their own good.

"You know, Wanda," said Cat kindly, "it's quite possible that when this whole exterminator thing blows over, a few of the mice will come back to stay."

"No," said Wanda taking a deep breath and looking determined, "it's best if they stay away. Miss Prattle will be on the lookout for them, and we can't risk even one mouse being harmed. But I certainly am going to miss the little dears. I've become quite fond of them." She picked up her purse and a stack of books from the circulation desk. "Well, I'll be going now," she said, trying to put on a brave face. "I still have to drop these books by Gladys Porter's house. Poor thing twisted her ankle and can't get around too well right now. I thought some bestsellers might help her pass the time."

"Oh, that reminds me," said Cat, opening the door for Wanda, who was loaded down with Gladys's potential reading material. "I ran into Basil Bramblewood the other night, and he said he saw a man stuffing something into the book drop next to the library stairs. Any idea what it was?"

"Oh, those were just the items Miss Prattle was expecting. They were a bit odd, though," said Wanda, looking perplexed. "I wonder what she needs with a food grinder and an old parchment map." She shrugged her shoulders, as she moved toward the door. "See you tomorrow afternoon," she said and headed off to the Porter's house.

After the library had closed for the evening, Catrina and Annie called another meeting of the mice.

"As some of you might have heard," began Catrina, looking around the basement, "the library is to be fumigated on Saturday. Therefore, Annie and I have taken the liberty of finding you all new living quarters. Bear in mind that you are in no way obligated to take up the living arrangements we have made for you, and if you prefer to make your own plans, you should feel free. However, for your own safety you must evacuate the premises by no later than nine o'clock on Friday. Annie and I will be here precisely at eight o'clock that evening to give you the addresses for your new living quarters and make certain that you and your belongings arrive safely at your destinations. Any questions?"

Albert's father stood on top of the cigar box his family called home and cleared his throat. "On behalf of all us mice," he said, "we just want to thank you for everything you have done for us, and we want you to know that if you ever need anything—anything at all—you only need ask. Our only concern at this point," he continued, "is Wanda. Since we have no way of communicating with her, we were hoping that you could find some way of letting her know how much we appreciate all the kindness she has shown us over the past months. We've become quite fond of her."

"I feel like I'm leaving my very best friend," sobbed one of the little girl mice. "She came down every morning to make sure we had enough mouse treats and to see if there were enough pieces of blanket to keep us warm at night. What if she doesn't know how much we love her?"

"I'm sure she knows," said Cat, a tear beginning to brim in the corner of her eye. "And I think you should know that she is quite fond of all of you as well." She looked over and saw Annie blotting her eyes with a handkerchief.

"So," said Cat, taking a deep breath and squaring her shoulders, "on with business. As hard as this might seem, if Wanda comes down here and begins trying to shoo you out, put on a good show and leave through the window. She's determined to get you all out before the exterminators from Rid a Rodent arrive. You can always use one of the outside tunnels to come back in later, but please try to stay out of Wanda's sight. It is imperative she thinks you have all gone. Also, please have your belongings together no later than seven thirty on Friday evening. As long as everyone is packed, things should go smoothly. Whiskers up, everyone, and we'll see you on Friday."

After Cat and Annie left, Albert slouched off and sat by himself in a corner of the basement.

Albert's father noticed his oldest son sitting alone in the dark and thought it was time the two had a heart-to-heart talk.

"You know, Albert," said his father, patting his son on the back, "this is not your fault. We all knew it was only a matter of time before some mortal found out we were here and called in the heavy artillery to have us removed. If it makes you feel any better, I spoke with Catrina earlier, and she said that after all this blows over, she's going to make sure the library tunnel is reopened, and you will be welcome to visit any time you like. She's even arranged for this." Albert's father produced a small piece of white plastic and placed it in his son's paw. On it was printed **A. Mouse**. "You're the first in our family," he said proudly, "perhaps even the first mouse in history, to have the privilege of owning his very own library card. I'm proud of you, son."

"I'm proud of you too, Dad," said Albert, giving his father a hug. But what Albert didn't say was that he had no intention of leaving.

6

Living Arrangements

The following morning Catrina and Annie met in the town's square. They planned to visit all those who had offered to house mice, thank them for their generosity, and make arrangements for each family.

Their first stop was Bianca Beechwood's health food store, Nature Knows Best.

The shop stood at the end of Main Street. It was a comfortable wood Victorian with a storybook front and inviting porch. The two window boxes facing the street were filled with geraniums, and the planters that stood on either side of the stairs spilled over with pink and white impatiens. Tucked into a corner of the porch was a small, cozy birdhouse painted to resemble a guest cottage, complete with a small sign that read "Bird and Bath". The porch was also home to a number of hanging baskets, a wheelbarrow that had been turned into a planter for an herb garden, and a couple of comfortable-looking white rockers.

The sign on the front door read *Open, Please Come In*, so Cat and Annie did just that.

"Bianca," called Catrina looking around for the proprietor. "Are you here?"

"I'm in the greenhouse. Come on back," called a voice from the back of the store. Cat and Annie made their way past the shelves of honey and whole grain breads to the glass structure attached to the shop. There they found Bianca studying a leaf covered with russet-colored spots.

"Aphids," she said, shaking her head. "The oleander is covered with them." She reached over to the plant and pinched off a few dry leaves. "Oh, well, guess it comes with the territory." She smiled. "What can I do for you two today?"

"We just came by to thank you for offering refuge to the library mice and make arrangements for their arrival," said Catrina.

"No problem," said Bianca, removing her gardening apron and hanging it on a peg by the door. "I'm looking forward to the levity they'll bring. Oh, by the way, I don't mean to play favorites, but do you think it would be possible for Albert's family to move in here? Their youngest girl, Emily, stops by to visit frequently, and we share interests. Do you know that little scamp can already identify thirty-seven types of plants by the seeds they drop? With a little training, that mouse could really go places."

"I think they'd be honored," said Catrina.

"Great." Bianca smiled. "I've already set up a couple of wooden crates for them in the corner near the periwinkle, and I've conjured up a portal that connects to the tunnel system. I think they'll be quite comfortable here."

"I'm sure they will," said Annie. "I just peeked in those crates." She turned to face Cat. "They're complete with wall-to-wall carpet, central heat and air, and an elevator that, if I'm not mistaken, goes up to Bianca's apartment above the shop."

"Well, what kind of hostess would I be if I let them get lonely?" Bianca winked as she pulled off her gardening gloves and laid them on a shelf next to the apron peg. "So where are you two off to now?"

"Crates of Critters," answered Annie.

"Hold up while I grab my sweater, and I'll go with you," said Bianca. "I need some insectivores."

Bianca grabbed her sweater, turned the store sign around to read *Closed, Please Call Again*, and the three made their way down the street to Carl Cunningham's pet shop.

When they arrived, Bailey Bramblewood and her best friend, Heather Gordon, were on their way out the door.

"Checking out the kittens?" Bianca questioned Bailey, smiling.

"I don't understand this girl," said Heather, who was a mortal. "Last month, my Persian, Biloxi Blue, had a litter of purebred kittens and we offered her the pick of the litter, free of charge, and she turned us down. Said she wasn't allowed until she turned twelve. My mom offered to talk to Mrs. Bramblewood and see if it would be OK since her birthday is only a few months away, but Miss Goody Two-Shoes here wouldn't hear of it."

Cat and Annie gave Bailey a knowing look. Bailey just smiled and shrugged her shoulders.

"Speaking of mothers," said Bailey, looking at Heather, "we promised yours we'd catch up to her in front of the post office, so we better hurry."

"See you later," said Cat, as the girls brushed by them on their way out of the store. "Bailey," called Cat, "would you do me a favor and tell your father the packages were nothing to be concerned about? He'll know what I'm referring to."

"Sure thing," called back Bailey, and the two girls disappeared around the corner.

"Good morning, ladies," came a cheerful voice from behind the counter near the front of the store. "What can I do for you today?"

"Hi, Carl," said Cat. "Annie and I came to talk to you about mouse lodging, but why don't you wait on Bianca first. She probably wants to get back to her store."

"Thanks," said Bianca. "I really do hate to close midmorning." She turned to Carl, who looked at her through his windshield-size glasses. "I'm having a problem with aphids," she said. "Do you happen to have any insectivores?"

"You're in luck," said Carl, walking around to the front of the counter. He turned the lock on the front door, flipped his *Open* sign to *Closed*, and pulled the shade down on the front window. "We just got an order of flibats in last night. I think they should do the trick." He made a circular motion with his hand in front of the wall behind the cash register, and a portal resembling the ones in the library basement, only larger, appeared. The four passed through and found themselves standing in another pet shop.

Carl led them past an aquarium of teacup-size dragons snoozing under sun lamps and back to a cage made of mosquito netting, which housed what at first glance appeared to be winged insects. He gently lifted the lid and placed his hand in the cage. Within seconds the small black creatures that had been flying around inside the cage landed on his index finger. He slowly removed them from the cage and presented them to Bianca.

Bianca held out her hand and seven bats no larger than flies crawled off Carl's finger and into her palm.

"The beauty of the flibat," said Carl, lowering the lid on the cage, "is that if they are spotted by a mortal, they are brushed off as common house flies. Of course I would be careful to keep them out of your main shop. It would be a shame to have someone swat one of the little guys."

"They're perfect," said Bianca, holding her palm to the end of her nose to have a closer look. "They'll fit right into the greenhouse. They can dine on aphids, and soon I'll be rid of spotted leaves. Thanks, Carl, I always know I can count on you for a solution. Could you please put them on my bill? I'm in a bit of a hurry to get back."

"Absolutely," said Carl, bowing as Bianca carefully placed the flibats in her sweater pocket and headed for the door.

"I'll be sure to turn the lock as I leave," said Bianca as she walked back through the portal. "Thanks again!"

"Now," said Carl, pushing his large glasses up higher onto his bulbous nose, "let's talk mice."

"Thank you," said Annie. "Do you have any preference as to what size family you'd like to house?"

"No, any size at all will be fine," answered Carl. "Just send me anyone you think would like it here. They'll be able to have free run of the shop back here, and if they happen to show up in the mortal shop area, no one will think anything of it. After all, this is a pet store."

Carl looked down at his feet, and Cat and Annie could not help but notice that the tips of his ears were turning pink.

"Uhmmmmmm, errr," he stammered. "Since the mice are leaving the library, do you think Wanda will still be stopping by for mouse treats?" he asked, while examining the tops of his shoes for imaginary specks of dust.

Cat and Annie exchanged smiles. They had suspected for some time that Wanda and Carl had a bit of a crush on each other, which was why Wanda kept purchasing small bags of mouse treats instead of the large jumbo bag. Smaller bags meant more trips to the store.

"Somehow, I think Wanda will still be needing a few mouse treats here and there," replied Cat, trying hard to sound serious. "After all, the mice will be coming back for visits. We issued Albert a library card, so we know he'll be back and forth borrowing and returning books."

"Oh, well, that's good," said Carl, a grin appearing on his face. "Now, if you ladies don't mind, I really should reopen the front shop."

"Not at all," said Annie, as she and Cat walked back through the portal and into the mortal shop. "Thanks again for helping out. The mice really appreciate it."

"My pleasure," said Carl. He waved his hand causing the portal to vanish, escorted his visitors to the front door, and flipped the *Closed* sign to *Open*. "If you need anything else, just let me know."

"Thank you, we will," said Cat, and she and Annie headed off to finish making their calls.

7

Evacuation

"Momma, I can't find Albert anywhere!" cried Albert's sister Emily from her perch on the windowsill.

It was the evening of the evacuation, and the library's basement was a madhouse. Mice were running everywhere as parents tried to account for children and confirm new living arrangements. To add to the confusion, two mice who had become engaged the previous week had picked that evening to elope, leaving their families to explain to relatives why they had not been invited to the wedding. The groom's grandmother, who was not taking the news well at all, kept spouting off about how mice today had no respect for their elders. The old mouse seemed intent on creating as horrible a scene as possible. Needless to say, while their parents' attention was focused on trying to smooth things over with Grandma, the adolescent mice seized the opportunity to get into as much mischief as possible. They were even holding contests to see who could create the most chaos.

"Edwin," called Albert's mother over the noise, "we still can't find Albert."

Albert's father looked up from dragging their cigar box toward one of the tunnels and called back, "Don't worry, Rose. He's probably just upstairs shrinking a few books for the trip."

Rose did not look convinced. Ever since it was announced that they would have to move, Albert had been acting strangely. He spent every spare minute in the children's library, and when Rose had gone searching for him the previous evening, she had found him sitting alone, staring up at the ceiling. She couldn't quite put her paw on exactly what was going on inside of her son's head, but she had a good idea he was planning something, and she wasn't sure she liked it.

"Ears up, everyone!" called Catrina, as she and Annie checked off names on clipboards.

The room fell silent. Even the adolescent mice gave up on their antics and settled back to listen.

"You should have all received your assignments by now. If you have not received your assignment, would you please raise a paw? Good. Now, if you'll pay attention, Annie has some information for you."

Annie stepped forward. "We have placed a shrinking spell on your possessions," she began, "which will reduce them to carrying size. We have also taken the liberty of providing you with wagons." Annie pointed to a corner of the basement where dozens of red mouse-size Radio Flyers stood ready and waiting. "The shrinking spell will automatically wear off in about three hours, at which time your things will return to their normal size, with the exception of the wagons, which we thought you might find more useful scaled down a bit. Please be advised that the tunnels will automatically seal in one hour and will stay that way for the remainder of the week. This is being done to make sure that no poisonous fumes reach into the transit system. We will reopen the portals after all danger has passed. When the portals are reopened, the library basement will act as your hub for the tunnel system. If you have any questions, Cat and I will be upstairs in the front lobby keeping an eye out for Miss Prattle. We're sure you'll enjoy your new homes, and remember, you're always welcome to visit."

"Thank you," yelled the mice.

"Tell Wanda we love her!" called a few of the younger mice.

Then, in perfect harmony, all the things belonging to the mice made a high, shrill noise and shrunk to sizes small enough to be carried by their owners.

For a moment everything was silent, then there was a flurry of activity, as the mice collected their families and belongings, loaded everything into wagons, and headed for the portals.

"Edwin, he's still not here!" called Albert's mother in a panic. "If we don't find him soon, he'll be sealed in."

"Calm down, Rose. We'll find him," answered Edwin, taking a head count to make sure everyone else was accounted for. "I'm sure he's around here somewhere." But if the truth were known, Albert's father was as worried as his wife. He wanted his family out and away from the threat of the exterminators, and he wanted them out now.

"I see him!" yelled Albert's younger sister Emily over the commotion. "He's on his way. It's OK!"

Just then, Rose and Edwin saw their oldest son running toward them through the crowd.

"Where have you been? We've been worried sick!" scolded his mother.

"It's all right, Rose. He's here now, and that's all that matters."

"Mom, Dad," said Albert, standing tall. "I'm not going."

"What do you mean, you're not going?" snapped Rose. Albert had found her last nerve and was stamping on it. "You collect your books and get in line right now, young man!"

"Mom," said Albert in a gentle but determined voice. "I love you and Dad very much, but this is my home, and I'm staying."

"But the exterminators – you'll be killed," said Albert's father. "Son, you need to think this through."

"I have, Dad," said Albert, staring his father directly in the eye. "I have a plan. Tonight, after everyone leaves, I'm going to crawl up the curtains, scale the cross beam on the ceiling, shimmy down the fishing line that holds the Mother Goose sculpture, and hide under her bonnet. The exterminators can't use anything that will cause fumes in the children's library because they might harm the kids, and if I'm suspended from the ceiling, they shouldn't be able to reach or find me. Dad, I love you and Mom very much, but this is my home and I'm staying. It's like you've always said, Dad, '*A mouse has got to do what a mouse has got to do.*'

"Oh, Edwin," cried Rose, dabbing at the tears that were beginning to spill from her eyes. "Our little boy is all grown up."

"It sounds like you're determined to stay," said Edwin, placing a paw on his son's shoulder. "Well, I guess there's nothing we can do to change your mind. Just remember, there's always a place for you in our cigar box, and there's never any shame in coming home."

"Thanks, Dad," said Albert.

He hugged his parents good-bye and headed off toward the stairs that led to the children's library.

"Albert, wait," came a small voice from the windowsill. It was Emily. She scurried down from her place on the ledge and ran to her brother.

"I heard what you said to Mom and Dad," she said, looking up at her brother with soft, brown eyes, "and I understand why you're staying. I haven't even moved into the greenhouse at Bianca's, and I already feel like it's my home. There's something very special that happens when you find your passion in life. For you, it's books. For me, it's plants. I never would have discovered my calling in life if you hadn't been patient and read me all those books on botany, and I just want you to know how much I appreciate it. Thank you, Albert." She hugged her brother, then hurried off to join the rest of their family.

Albert felt a tug at his heart as he watched his family disappear through one of the portals. He stood and watched until they were out of sight, then he took a deep breath and hurried up the stairs to hide.

8

The Mouse Detector

Albert hardly had time to squeeze under the floppy blue bonnet that rested on top of Mother Goose's head before Catrina and Annie came in from their lookout post accompanied by Bailey and Braden Bramblewood.

"Thanks for taking us along tonight, Annie," said Braden, walking over to the circulation desk.

Annie was going owl-watching later that night and had invited Braden and Bailey to tag along.

"You're quite welcome," said Annie. "The more the merrier when it comes to owl-watching."

Bailey, who was a few paces behind her brother, stopped and looked carefully around.

"Miss Prattle isn't here, is she?" questioned Bailey nervously. "I saw a light on in her office as we were coming up the sidewalk. If she finds us here after hours, she'll scold us for sure."

"Don't worry," said Catrina. "Miss Prattle's nowhere around. The light you saw is one she keeps on a plant in her office."

"What kind of plant?" asked Bailey.

"I've no idea," answered Cat. "She never lets anyone near it. But whatever it is, it's growing at an amazing rate. Yesterday, when I walked by her office, I could see one of its vines trying to creep out under the crack at the bottom of the door."

"She's an odd one, that woman," said Annie, shaking her head, and the others nodded in agreement.

"Oh, before I forget," said Braden, reaching into his pocket and producing a small silver disc. "Look what I brought. It's a mouse detector. I made it myself. Now we'll be able to make sure all the mice are out."

"What a wonderful idea," said Annie examining the disc. "How does it work?"

Braden walked over to the stairs and tossed the disc into the basement. It began making a humming noise as it spun in the air.

"It just flies around and checks all the cracks and corners for stray mice," said Braden, returning to the desk.

"If it detects a mouse, it beeps. I was going to have it play "Three Blind Mice," but a certain someone wouldn't let me." He raised an eyebrow at his sister, who stood glaring back at him.

"If you were a mouse, don't you think you'd find the part about having your *tail cut off with a carving knife* just a tad bit disturbing?" questioned Bailey crossly.

"Well, on to other things," said Annie, hoping to stave off an argument between the siblings. "Did you both remember to bring your owl identification notebooks?"

"Right here!" said Braden, patting his knapsack.

Albert, who was spying down from a loose seam underneath Mother Goose's blue bonnet, began to tremble. It was unnerving enough waiting to see if that humming flying saucer was going to give him away, but now he had to listen to talk about owls. Albert was extremely frightened of owls and for good reason. Owls eat mice. Albert knew that all mice were frightened of owls, so he was not in the least bit embarrassed by his fear. After all, he had grown up hearing stories of how even the most stalwart of mice had fainted dead away just upon seeing an owl, only to end up as its dinner. Why on earth, he wondered, would anyone go out looking for owls? He was just thinking to himself that he would much rather take his chances alone with the exterminators than to be out in the woods with the others when he heard the soft hum of the mouse detector. He watched, motionless, as it flew back up the stairway and hovered precariously over the circulation desk. It began to rise slightly and Albert was certain it was going to give his position away, and it probably would have, if Braden hadn't chosen just that moment to reach out and grab it.

"Looks like the basement's all clear," he announced, pocketing the disc.

"Great," said Annie, picking up her sweater. "Everyone ready to go?"

"Absolutely," said Bailey, smiling at the others.

Albert watched as they turned off the lights and closed the library doors. He heard the clicking of the lock as they turned the key in the outside door and listened to their footsteps as they clattered down the cement stairs and onto the street below. Then everything was eerily quiet.

Albert felt his stomach tie up in knots as he realized there was no warm cigar box waiting for him in the corner of the basement, no parents to scold him for being late, and no brothers and sisters waiting to be crawled over on his way to bed. Nor were there aunts and uncles waiting to question him about his adventures in the upper part of the building, or cousins begging him to join them in a game of *mousecapades*. He clutched his tail between his paws, took a deep breath, and realized that for the first time in his life, he was completely alone.

9

Rid a Rodent Cometh

Albert awoke the next morning to the shrill sound of Miss Prattle's voice.

"I want you to check everywhere. Everywhere, do you hear me?" came the icy voice of the Library Director. "If I see one of those awful rodents after you've left, I'll have your jobs, don't think I won't!"

"Very well, miss," came a rather gruff reply from one of the two men who were now entering the children's library.

"Have our jobs indeed" chuckled the other, as they lay down two large burlap bags full of equipment. "Would be a bit hard for her to do seein' as how we own the company and all, eh George?"

"Got that right, Fred," replied the larger of the two. "Wonder what those mice did to get her that mad at them. Don't suppose she's trying to eliminate competition for the world's most pointed nose award, do you?" The two shared a laugh while unloading their equipment.

"So where'd you want to start?" asked Fred.

"Basement, I suppose," answered George. "Then we'll do the children's library and head on upstairs to the second floor. She wants everything done but her office. Said she was going to lock it and leave. Look, there she goes now."

The two men watched from the window as Miss Prattle crossed the street. She stopped to kick at a squirrel who was burying a nut in the soft earth next to the sidewalk, then ran to catch up with a thin man who was wearing a dark coat, which was rather peculiar considering it was quite warm out.

"She's an odd one, that one," said George, pulling a canister out of one of the bags. "Wonder what her story is."

"Don't think I care to know," grumbled Fred. "I'm just hoping she never has to call us back. I got a bad feeling about that one. It's like she hasn't got a heart at all."

"Know what you mean," said George, attaching a spray wand to the end of one of the canisters. "Know just what you mean."

The two finished assembling their equipment, put protective overalls on over their blue jeans and t-shirts, strapped the canisters to their backs, and headed down the stairs. It wasn't long before Albert could hear the hissing noise of the sprayers, as the men released deadly chemicals into the basement's interior.

Albert could not decide what to do. He knew the men couldn't possibly use spray chemicals above the basement because they could be harmful to humans, but he was no longer certain that hiding out under Mother Goose's bonnet was such a good idea. He could just barely smell the fumes coming up the library stairs and his head was starting to pound. He finally decided his best chance for survival was to make his way to the second floor and squeeze under the crack of Miss Prattle's locked office door. The thought of entering Miss Prattle's office didn't set well with him, but he decided it was preferable to being gassed.

Albert waited until he could hear the men moving along the far side of the basement wall, took a deep breath, and made a run for the fishing line that held the soft sculpture in place. After scaling the line, he raced along the crossbeam and headed for the air vent. Once inside the vent, he had to decide whether to go right or left. This was an extremely important decision, as one way would lead up to the safety of the second floor while the other would lead him toward the deadly fumes in the basement.

Perhaps I should rethink this, he thought, but it was too late. He stared out of the dark vent as Fred and George, who didn't seem like such bad sorts with the exception that they killed mice, came traipsing up the basement stairs.

"Close the door behind ya, Fred," called George, as he emerged from the basement. "Then we'll pack up the sprayers and check the ductwork for anything that might be hiding in there."

Albert's heart skipped a beat. He turned to his left and inched slowly along, feeling for the smooth metal in front of him. He was just becoming a bit braver with his movements when one of his paws stepped down into nothingness. He wobbled back and forth trying to regain his balance, but the metal was slippery, and he began sliding downward. He could smell the toxic fumes below him and was certain that he was about to meet his end.

Then, just as all hope seemed to be gone, he felt something scratch his ear. He reached out just in time to catch the head of a screw with his right front paw. He hung there in silence with only the screw's head standing between him and certain doom.

Albert took a deep breath, mustered all of his strength, and began pulling his body upward. He pulled up as far as he could with his right front paw while feeling for the flat surface above his head with the left. When he found it, he used every ounce of his strength to throw the top part of his body onto the horizontal surface. He then placed a back paw on the screw's head and pushed the rest of his body onto the cool flat metal. He lay there for a moment, exhausted, then forced himself back onto his feet and went in search of a way up. He had only to go a few feet before the ductwork made a sharp turn upward. He was wondering how he was going to make it up the smooth sides when he noticed that there were screws placed about every two inches. Grasping the heads of the screws, he climbed paw over paw until he came to another vent opening and squeezed through the grate.

Albert looked around. He couldn't believe his eyes. There was shelf after shelf of books stacked almost to the ceiling. *So*, he thought, *this is the adult library*. He was just about to take a look around when he heard footsteps on the stairwell and remembered why he was there.

He raced quickly down the hallway, looking for Miss Prattle's office. There were many closed doors along the corridor that he could have easily squeezed underneath, but he knew the exterminators would enter all of them with the exception of Prattle's, which was locked. He searched right and left, looking for clues that would tell him which office belonged to the beady-eyed director, but from the outside, they all looked alike. He stopped just long enough to catch his breath, and that's when he saw it. Directly in front of him, creeping out from the crack at the bottom of a door, were the green leaves of a plant. *That's it*, he said to himself. *That's her office*! He ran to the door and squeezed underneath, just as Fred and George from Rid a Rodent entered the hallway.

Albert leaned back on the office door, closed his eyes, and complimented himself on how he, Albert, mouse extraordinaire, had managed to outsmart not one, but two of Rid a Rodent's finest. He was daydreaming about the story he would tell his cousins when he suddenly had a bad feeling that something was watching him. Albert opened his eyes and could not believe what he saw. The leaves curling out from under the office door were only offshoots of a much larger plant that had all but taken over the small room. The long, dark vine, which oddly appeared to be thicker toward its ends than its center, had large, green, oval-shaped leaves with yellow, hourglass-shaped spots that occasionally curled back into themselves, only to sprout out again in new directions. As if this weren't enough, every two feet or so there emerged from this chaos a black tendril that was tipped with blossoms of purple, yellow, and orange. The vine sprawled along the wall, across the mahogany desk, behind a gold nameplate that read P. Prattle, Director of Services in black gothic-style letters, and onto a shelf with a strange-looking lamp. Albert followed it with his eyes, looking for its point of origin and almost fell over as he realized that the entire abundance of leaf, vine, and blossom all sprouted from a pot no larger than a thimble.

How is that possible? he wondered. He remembered Emily showing him several picture books that boasted a variety of houseplants. She had even pointed out several varieties of philodendron to him that she had found in a copy of *A Child's Guide to House Plants*, but all of those plants were properly potted in containers that matched their size, and none of them harbored the menacing quality that this plant seemed to possess. Something wasn't right here.

Albert was standing staring at the plant and picking nervously at the end of his tail when Fred passed by the door and caught the toe of his shoe on the leaves that had spilled out into the hallway.

"Hey, George," yelled Fred, kicking at the leaves and sounding agitated. "Are you goin' to take all day or what?" Fred did not know what had come over him, but suddenly he felt angry.

"Be done in just a minute," came an answer from down the hall. "Somethin' wrong?"

"No, just don't feel like hanging around here all day while you take your own sweet time is all," called Fred, a

definite edge to his voice. He pulled his foot away from
the plant and immediately began to feel like himself again.

"Well no need to get mad," called George gruffly.
"I'm workin' as fast as I can. What's your problem
anyway? You feelin' OK? You look a little peaked."

"Yeah, I'm fine. At least I am now, anyway. Sorry,
George, I don't know what got into me. It's like all of a
sudden I was just kinda mad at the world."

"It's OK," said George, holding the elevator door
open so the two could load their equipment. "It's been a
rough day, having to deal with the dragon lady and all.
And who knows, maybe you caught some fumes. We're
through here. Let's call it a day."

Albert listened for the elevator's doors to close
before crawling cautiously out into the hallway. He
climbed the curtains next to the stacks and watched from
the window until the yellow van with Rid a Rodent painted
professionally on its side pulled away from the curb.
Then, exhausted from the excitement of the day, he made
his way down to the children's library. He sniffed the air
to make certain it was clear of fumes, then scaled the
crossbeam that led to the fishing line from which the soft

sculpture was suspended. He slid down the fishing line onto Mother Goose's back and slipped quietly under her blue bonnet, where he curled up into a small ball and tried hard not to think about whatever it was that was growing in Miss Prattle's office.

10

Emily Spills the Beans

Brothers can be so worrisome, thought Emily as she sat on the roof of her family's crate in Bianca's greenhouse. When she had first heard Albert say he was going to stay in the library she had thought it was no big deal, but now she wasn't so sure. Her parents had done nothing but pace the floor since they had left him, and she herself kept having images of her poor brother lying in some dark corner gasping for breath as the exterminators performed their duties.

"Emily, is everything all right?" questioned Bianca, as she stood pruning the periwinkle in the greenhouse. "I haven't seen you smile once since you arrived, and your parents haven't ventured out of your family's crate at all. You did want to stay here, didn't you? I mean, if you don't, you needn't feel obligated. I'd miss you, of course, but I'd understand."

Emily bit her bottom lip and tugged nervously at her whiskers.

"Bianca, if I tell you something—something really important—do you promise to keep it a secret?"

"Well, I'll do my best, of course," answered Bianca, looking quite serious. "It depends on the secret. Emily, what has you so upset?"

"Albert," wailed Emily. "He's still in the library. He refused to leave. He was going to try to ride out the extermination under Mother Goose's bonnet. Oh, Bianca, we're so frightened for him!"

"As well you should be!" gasped Bianca. "What did he think he was doing? We'd better call Catrina right away. I'm sure she'll open the library so I can check on him."

"Let me go with you, please!" begged Emily.

"OK," said Bianca, pulling off her gardening gloves and placing them on a shelf, "but first tell your parents you're leaving. They have enough to worry about without you going missing."

Emily ran into the crate to tell her parents she would be going out for a while, then climbed up Bianca's arm and hid beneath her long, chestnut hair.

Bianca grabbed her copy of the *Western District Witches Directory*, dialed Catrina's number, and was relieved when her call was answered on the second ring.

"Cat, this is Bianca. I hate to bother you on a Sunday, but I'm afraid we have a bit of a situation here. It appears that Albert managed to get himself locked in the library over the weekend."

"Albert? Are you certain?" questioned Catrina, sounding more than a little alarmed.

"Yes, apparently he was hiding in the soft sculpture in the children's section. Emily just told me. The poor thing is frantic."

"Braden swept the basement for mice before we left on Friday," said Catrina. "Obviously, we should have checked the entire building. I'll phone the Bramblewoods and have Braden bring the mouse detector and meet us at the back entrance. Tell Emily to try to stay calm. If he's in there, we'll find him."

Bianca hung up the phone and grabbed her sweater. Ten minutes later, the small group was assembled at the back entrance to the library.

Catrina fumbled through her purse and found the key to the door. Once inside, Braden pulled the mouse detector from his pocket and gave it a toss. It hung in the air in front of him and began humming softly as it spun. Then, suddenly, it took off.

The group followed silently behind the detector as it flew into the children's library and circled the story corner. It hovered briefly over the soft sculpture of Mother Goose, then took a nosedive and came to rest on the circulation desk, where it began to beep.

There they found Albert, lying on his side on the mouse pad next to the computer terminal.

"Albert, are you all right?" asked Bianca, poking the small mouse in the side.

"Thank goodness! We thought you might be dead!" gasped Catrina, as Albert bolted upright.

"Albert," squeaked Emily, who was obviously relieved her beloved big brother was alive and well. "What are you doing down here? I thought you were going to hide in the soft sculpture."

Albert had tried hard to stay put under the droopy, blue bonnet perched on Mother Goose's head, but every time a stray thread brushed him he jumped, imagining it to be a tendril from the vine growing in Prattle's office. He finally decided to park himself on the circulation desk, where he could keep an eye on things and, out of exhaustion, had fallen asleep. He knew he should tell them this, but somehow he just couldn't bring himself to admit that he had braved the exterminators only to be frightened by a plant.

"Well, this is a mouse pad," answered Albert, sounding quite full of himself, "and I am, after all, a mouse."

"A lucky-to-be-alive mouse!" scolded Catrina. "Honestly, Albert, sometimes I wonder about you." Cat shook her head. "Well, I guess as long as I'm here, I may as well check out the basement and see if it's safe to reopen the tunnels." She turned to Albert. "You stay here. We're going to have a little talk when I get back."

"Albert, I'm glad you're all right," said Braden, pocketing his mouse detector. "Cat, I have to leave. Mom and Dad wanted me to hurry right back." He winked at Albert and left, closing the door behind him.

Bianca set Emily down next to her brother, then went off to help Cat make certain the basement was clear of fumes.

"Mom and Dad are beside themselves," Emily told Albert. "If they reopen the tunnels, I'll run home and let them know you're all right."

"Thanks," said Albert clutching his tail between his paws.

A few minutes later, Cat and Bianca returned.

"The basement's safe," announced Cat, "and the tunnels are open. Albert, I take it you hid out because you want to live here, is that correct?" she questioned sternly.

"Yes, ma'am," said Albert, clutching his tail even harder.

"Well, you're welcome to stay, but you must promise never to pull another stunt like this one. In the future, if you have a problem, you come to one of us with it. Is that clear?"

"Yes, ma'am," said Albert, dropping his tail and giving a sigh of relief.

Something inside Albert told him he should tell Catrina about the strange vine that had all but taken over

Miss Prattle's office. About how it seemed evil and had given him nightmares, but somehow it just seemed too unmousely to be frightened of a plant.

"You two run along to the basement now," said Cat, picking up the mice and setting them gently on the floor. "Bianca and I are going by Annie's to fill her in on the happenings here."

Once downstairs, Albert felt a little uneasy. It was dark and a bit damp in the basement, and after Emily left there would be no one to keep him company.

"Albert, are you sure you're going to be all right here?" questioned Emily. "Somehow it doesn't seem so cozy with everyone gone."

"I'll be fine," said Albert, sounding braver than he felt. "You get along home and let Mom and Dad know I'm OK."

"All right," said Emily. She gave her brother a quick hug and disappeared into one of the tunnels.

Albert was exhausted. It was getting late, and he had slept very little over the weekend. He tried making himself a nest in an abandoned flowerpot filled with shredded tissue, but he just couldn't seem to get comfortable. Finally, he went back upstairs in search of a book to shrink. When he returned, he saw a small red wagon with a box sitting in it by one of the portals. He walked over and lifted the box out of the back of the wagon. When he placed it on the ground, it began to tremble and make a high, shrill noise. Then there was a popping sound, and Albert couldn't believe what appeared. There, sitting in front of him, lined with the same kind of ABC paper that he had learned to read from, was his family's cigar box with a note pinned to its side that read:

> Dear Albert,
>   Mom was worried about you and thought you might like the family cigar box. She said to tell you that Bianca has outfitted us with individual matchboxes inside our crate, so you needn't feel guilty about accepting it.
>   We miss you already.
>   Love,
>   Emily

Albert folded the note and placed it under his arm. Then he pushed the cigar box under the windowsill where it was washed by moonlight, settled into its familiar surroundings, and fell asleep with a book in his arms.

11

The Invitation

June bloomed in Harborville, and with the ushering in of the warm weather came the letting out of school for summer break. This event caused the McFarlands' collie, Andrew, to change his post from in front of the elementary school to the corner of First and Main. This was the street corner crossed by the children attending the town's summer preschool program on Tuesdays, as they traveled straight from splash dancing at the Harborville public pool to the lower level of the library for story and activity hour.

Annie, who was very energetic and always filled with enthusiasm, took great delight in playing hostess to the children who attended the program, and there was always great fun to be had. There were books to read, puzzles to put together, and even the occasional scavenger hunt—usually brought about by a misplaced sweater or backpack.

Of the fifteen children who attended the program, three were witches, which sometimes made for a rather unique set of situations. Like the time Patsy Peterson hiccupped and turned Freddie Caulfield into a bullfrog. Freddie returned to his old self in the blink of an eye, as the magic that is conjured by the very young is both unintentional and short lived. He did, however, insist on hopping to the car when his mother arrived to pick him up and then proceeded to croak every fifteen minutes or so for the remainder of the afternoon, a condition his mother chalked up to a gassy stomach. It was after this event that Bailey graciously agreed to help keep an eye on things and became the library's first story hour volunteer.

On this particular Tuesday afternoon, Annie's enthusiasm was exceeded by Bailey's.

"We're going!" Bailey whispered excitedly to Annie and Catrina, as she came through the library doors carrying paper cutouts of farm animals for the afternoon's craft project.

"Going where?" inquired Cat, knowing full well the answer.

"To Witchfest!" exclaimed Bailey. "Dad surprised us with the news right after dinner last night. He's taking our whole family: Mom, me, Braden! Why, he's even asked Aunt Tildy to come along!" Aunt Tildy was Mrs. Bramblewood's sister and a frequent visitor to the Bramblewood home. "It's going to be great!"

"I'm sure it will be," Cat smiled, "and here's a little something that might make it even better." She slipped Bailey a clipping from the *Witch's Weekly News.*

Witchfest 2,303 is just around the corner, and here's the latest scoop from the Dark Caverns of Hanhoo. It appears as though Hildegard Harrowitz, the High Witch herself, will be making an appearance. Hildegard and her cat, Charm, will be on hand for the opening ceremonies and will also be offering seminars. Space is limited, so all those wishing to attend one of Ms. Harrowitz's seminars should get their reservations in early.

The article was accompanied by a picture of the High Witch herself, seated on a blue velvet chair with her Snow Bengal cat, Charm, perched majestically by her side.

Hildegard Harrowitz was Bailey Bramblewood's idol and one of the few witches talented enough to pair up with a Snow Bengal. You see, one reason a cat has to agree to a pairing is because the type and power of magic a witch can produce has a great deal to do with his or her cat. A Bengal and a witch, when properly paired, can produce some very powerful magic indeed, and a witch paired with a Snow Bengal can produce the most powerful magic of all. Needless to say, there are few witches who are chosen by Snow Bengals, as it takes a particularly gifted witch to handle this pairing properly.

Bailey looked at the snow-white cat with its black, rosette spots and blue eyes staring out from the photograph and nearly melted. Never could she remember having seen anything more beautiful.

"They're going to be there! They're really going to be there!" exclaimed Bailey, hardly breathing. "I can't wait! Do you think I'll get a chance to meet them?"

"Oh, I think there's a possibility your paths could cross," said Annie, as she picked up an armful of books from the circulation desk and headed to the rocking chair in the children's corner. She winked over her shoulder at Cat, who was wearing an impish grin.

Bailey carefully folded the clipping, placed it in her pants pocket, and took her place on the soft rug, where she could keep an eye on her charges.

Albert, who was always in the mood for a good story, had made his way up the basement stairs and was quietly perched on the windowsill just out of sight behind the blue cotton curtains.

He sat quietly, listening contentedly to the stories. Then, when the kids were busy with their activity, he crawled cautiously up the back of the curtains onto the crossbeam and into the venting system, where he made his way to the floor above. He had been making this trip twice a week, ever since he'd discovered the odd-looking plant that had given him nightmares. He hated being on the same floor, rather less in the same room with the thing, but he had once heard the saying *"keep your friends close and your enemies closer,"* and as far as Albert was concerned, the plant growing in Prattle's office was definitely the enemy.

On the positive side, Miss Prattle had taken to pruning the plant so that it no longer crept out from underneath the door, which meant Albert no longer had to scale the dreadful thing to make his way into the office.

Albert knew that it was common practice for people to prune plants, so the fact that Miss Prattle had taken to snipping at the vines with a pair of stainless steel scissors did not surprise him. What he did find surprising was that Miss Prattle couldn't seem to bring herself to part with the cuttings. She never threw them away, nor did she place them in water to root and sprout new plants. Instead, she carefully removed the leaves and placed them in a large brass bowl she kept beside her desk. Then, after they had dried for a few days, she ground them up in a device that greatly resembled a pepper mill.

Albert found this behavior strange, but not nearly as strange as the fact that Miss Prattle had been grinding up leaves for nearly two weeks and had hardly produced enough powder to cover the bottom of a small glass jar that she apparently kept just for this purpose. But then, reasoned Albert, if the massive plant that occupied the office could spring from a thimble-size pot, why should it be so astonishing that when ground up, it was hardly enough to see? As far as Albert could tell, the entire thing defied all logic.

Meanwhile, downstairs in the children's library, activity hour was coming to an end. Everything had gone smoothly, with the exception of one tricky moment when Patsy Peterson had sneezed, causing her animal cutouts to go berserk and begin to moo, cluck, and oink. Luckily Bailey, who was a very quick thinker, had covered quite cleverly by breaking into a chorus of "Old McDonald Had a Farm," and everyone had joined in. As luck would have it, what the preschoolers lacked in talent they more than made up for in volume, and the cutouts were drowned out by the cheerful, off-key voices of the singers.

Albert arrived back in the children's library just as the last child was being picked up. He saw Bailey standing at the circulation desk and decided to stop and say hello.

"Did you hear the news?" asked Bailey excitedly, as Albert took his place on the mouse pad next to the computer. "Dad's taking our whole family to Witchfest 2,303."

"Well, that's wonderful," said Albert, wondering to himself just exactly what one did at a Witchfest.

"And guess who's going to be there!" exclaimed Bailey. "Hildegard Harrowitz and Charm."

Albert had heard of the High Witch, Hildegard Harrowitz and her Snow Bengal, Charm, but he had no idea they were anything to become so excited about.

"Why, that's wonderful!" exclaimed Albert, trying to sound excited so as not to put a damper on Bailey's enthusiasm.

Cat, who was sitting at the circulation desk checking in books, suddenly had an idea. She reached down and picked up the small mouse. "Albert," she said, "the library is going to be closed for painting and roof repairs near the end of August, so Annie and I are taking Eve and Paisley and going to Witchfest. It's bound to be lonely around here with everyone gone. Would you like to come with us?"

Albert did not have to be asked twice. Finding out what one did at a Witchfest was much more appealing than being left alone with Prattle's plant for a week.

"Why, thank you," said Albert. "I'd love too."

"I have to run," said Bailey. "I promised Mom I'd help her with some canning potions. I'm glad you're coming to Witchfest, Albert," she called over her shoulder as she slipped through the door.

"Bye," called Cat and Annie after her. "Thanks for your help."

They watched from the window as Bailey crossed the street.

"What do you think, is now a good time?" asked Cat, turning to Annie.

"As good as any!" Annie grinned.

They watched Bailey stop in her tracks as a blue satin envelope tied with a silver ribbon miraculously appeared in her hand. Bailey carefully opened it and let out a squeal as she read its contents.

Bailey Bramblewood is cordially invited
to attend a seminar presented by
Hildegard Harrowitz
"Pairing with A Cat: What Every Witch Should Know"
at Witchfest 2,303
Date and time to be announced.
The courtesy of a reply is respectfully requested.

12
Witchfest

Summer sped by as if being chased, and before anyone could quite believe it, the calendar announced that it was nearing the end of August and time for Witchfest 2,303 to get underway.

Cat and Annie were in the library, making certain that things were put away properly for the week the library would be closed, when Wanda came gliding cheerfully through the door. "Hello, all," she chirped, as she waltzed into the room. "How is everyone this morning? Ready for a week's vacation, I hope. I know I certainly am."

"Absolutely," said Cat with a broad smile. "And how about you? Are you ready for your week at the beach? I hope you have sunscreen in that bag." She nodded at the brown parcel Wanda was holding.

Wanda looked around to make sure the three were alone, lowered her voice, and said in a conspiratorial tone. "Actually, I have mouse treats in the bag." She leaned in closer and lowered her voice even more. "I don't know if you're aware of this, but we still have one mouse."

Cat and Annie tried their best to look surprised at Wanda's news.

"The little dear is living in the basement in an old cigar box. I've been feeding him for a while now. You really should see him. He's quite cute and very tame. He takes mouse treats right out of my hand and then squeaks just as if to say thank you."

Cat and Annie couldn't tell Wanda, but that was exactly what Albert was saying. Albert had told them how Wanda had found him sleeping in his cigar box one morning and had made it a point to make certain that he was well fed. Albert appreciated Wanda's efforts, and being the polite, well-bred mouse that he was, he always squeaked his thanks for the food she brought him.

"Anyway, I was afraid the poor little thing would get hungry while we were gone, so I thought I'd leave a little extra food out before we closed up."

"You didn't happen to run into Carl Cunningham when you were picking up those mouse treats, did you?" asked Annie, winking at Cat.

The two witches watched as Wanda turned bright pink.

"As a matter of fact, I did run into him," answered Wanda, looking down at the brown bag she was cradling on her hip. "He asked me to dinner week after next."

Cat and Annie smiled happily, as Wanda nearly floated down the basement stairs. When she returned, she told her friends good-bye, then went to meet Gladys so they could head off to the beach.

"Albert, are you ready to go?" called Cat down the stairs. "Eve and Annie's cat, Paisley, are getting impatient."

Albert scurried up the basement stairs. "Yes. Sorry it took me so long, but I wanted to take the mouse treats Wanda left me to Mom and Dad's so they wouldn't go to waste. How are we getting there, anyway?"

"We're taking Annie's Volkswagen Beetle," answered Cat. "Now hop in my pocket, and let's get going."

Albert did as he was told, and the group made its way out to the back parking lot, where they all piled into

Annie's Volkswagen, drove to her house, and promptly parked in the garage.

"What are we stopping for?" asked Albert, who was both excited and a bit nervous to be going so far from home.

"Just a few preparations for our flight," said Cat, patting the small mouse on the head.

"Flight?" questioned Albert. "I thought you said we were taking Annie's Volkswagen."

"We are," said Cat, looking down at Albert, "but you certainly don't expect us to drive all the way to the Caverns of Hanhoo, do you? Why, that would take days."

Albert watched as Cat and Annie popped the trunk of the light orange car and pulled out two large magnetic black dots, which they placed on the outside of the car's doors. They then retrieved a large black semicircle and placed it above the front fender.

"That should do it," said Annie, admiring their work. "Now just a little shrinking spell and we'll be on our way. Cat, would you please do the honors?"

"Glad to," said Cat. "Now, let's see. Oh yes, I've got it: 'The Caverns of Hanhoo are awaiting our call, so make this package oh, so small.'"

"Oh, that was cute," said Annie a bit sarcastically, as she picked up Albert.

"Well, if you want poetry, you have to give me more notice," said Cat, as she tucked her short, blond hair behind her ears.

She and Cat hopped into the front seats and waited for the familiar shrill, whistling noise that accompanied a shrinking spell.

Albert felt an odd sensation in his stomach as the car and its contents, himself included, shook for a moment, then shrank to the size of a small bug.

"OK, we're off!" said Annie, laughing as she turned the ignition. Annie stepped on the gas, but instead of the car rambling off toward the garage door, it glided easily into the air, banked left, and sped through a small crack in the corner of the ceiling.

Albert, who was sitting on the dashboard staring wide-eyed out the windshield, was simply flabbergasted.

"You see, Albert," explained Cat, "if anyone sees us, they'll think we're a ladybug."

"What if someone takes a swat at us?" questioned Albert, clutching his tail tightly between his paws.

"They'd miss. It's part of the charm of the shrinking spell," answered Annie. "Just sit back and enjoy the ride. It's an absolutely glorious day to be flying!"

Albert couldn't argue that. The skies were the bluest he'd ever seen, and occasionally Annie would fly above the clouds, leaving a cotton candy carpet below. It was only a matter of minutes before Albert relaxed and decided that flying was the most exhilarating experience he had ever had the pleasure of knowing, and it seemed all too soon when Cat pointed out a dark mountain range looming in the distance.

"We're almost there," she announced. "Time to put on your seatbelts and prepare to land."

Annie studied the mountain range for a moment, then zeroed in on the third mountain from the left. She hovered in the air for a moment, then made a circular motion with her hand and conjured a portal.

Annie flew directly into the portal and set the Volkswagen down on what looked to be a small runway. As the car taxied along, Albert once again felt a strange sensation in his stomach, and the next thing he knew, the car and its contents, himself included, were full-size and driving along a tunnel where signs directed them to different parking areas.

"Let's see," said Cat, retrieving a set of tickets from her purse. "We're on level seven, tunnel five, cavern three. There it is just ahead, and look, there's valet parking."

Albert watched as the car in front of them floated up to a parking area and hung magically in the air.

Annie pulled the car up to the entrance of the tunnel, and the passengers poured out.

"Here comes our instructional bubble," purred Eve.

Albert looked upward and saw a shimmering, translucent ball descending toward them. Cat waited until it was above their heads then instructed everyone to "Listen up." She then reached up and popped the filmy sphere with her thumb.

"Welcome to Witchfest 2,303," said a voice. "Please pick up your directional rings from your host or hostess prior to entering the caverns. We hope you enjoy your stay."

Cat placed Albert on her shoulder where he could take in the sights, and they all went to stand in line with the other Witchfest-goers waiting to have their tickets checked.

"Cat, Annie!" came an excited voice from near the front of the line. It was Bailey. She was standing with her parents, her brother, and Aunt Tildy. "We were hoping we'd run into you soon. Sebastian has been driving Braden crazy wanting to know when Eve and Paisley were going to get here."

Albert looked over and saw that Eve and Paisley had spied Sebastian. The small mouse watched a bit nervously as the three cats went off to mingle with the other felines that were milling around in front of the entrance.

The line leading into the caverns moved quickly, and it was only a matter of minutes before Cat and Annie were greeted by their host.

"Welcome to Witchfest," said a rather rotund witch with dark hair and a handlebar moustache. He presented a velvet cushion that held two rings with compass settings. "If you will please place your directional rings on your right index fingers, you may continue on to your rooms. Your suite is down tunnel five and to your left. Your luggage will arrive shortly. We hope you have a wonderful stay."

Albert watched as Cat and Annie placed the rings on their fingers and headed into the caverns.

"What are the rings for?" questioned Albert, scurrying down Cat's sleeve to admire the jewelry that graced her finger.

"They're directional rings," answered Cat, touching the top of the compass and admiring the silver needlepoint that was set in a fourteen-karat gold band. "They help you to get around and keep you from becoming lost. Here, I'll show you how it works. The suite of Annie Arkinson and Catrina Cantwick, please," said Cat, holding her hand in front of her.

Albert watched as the delicate silver point on the compass swirled around several times, then came to a stop pointing straight in front of them.

"We just follow the arrow," said Cat, "and it will direct us to wherever we ask."

Cat and Annie checked in back of them to make certain that Eve and Paisley were following, then proceeded to walk down the tunnel. When they came to a fork, Cat lifted her hand and the silver arrow pointed left. They followed the arrow and soon arrived at a tunnel with doors on either side, some of which had informational bubbles suspended above them. They continued walking down the hall until the silver compass arrow pointed to one of the entrances. There they stopped and popped another filmy sphere that hung just above their heads.

"Welcome to your suite," came a charming-sounding voice. "For your convenience, we have had your luggage placed in your rooms. If you require any assistance, please call the front desk. We do hope you enjoy your stay."

Cat and Annie opened the door and walked into their suite, which consisted of a cozy living room complete with fireplace, a fully equipped kitchen, a dining room nicely appointed with an oak table and chairs, and two large bedrooms.

"Well, this looks comfy," said Cat, taking a look around. She set down her purse and placed Albert on the ground with Eve and Paisley. "Now you three can go investigate, but please don't leave the suite just yet. We don't want Albert getting lost."

"Don't worry, we'll look after him," purred Eve, and the three took off to explore their new surroundings.

13

Hats, Brooms, and Capes

Albert spent his first night in the caverns tossing and turning. He dreamed that Prattle's plant had found him and wrapped him in its vines. No matter how he moved, he couldn't seem to free himself from its clutches. When he finally woke, he found that he had managed to wrap himself mummy-style in the mouse-size sheets and blanket Cat had given him.

He scurried into the kitchen for breakfast, anxious to put the nightmare behind him. There he found Cat and Annie, dressed in what he assumed were witches' garments. They sported long, black dresses, complete with capes that draped past their shoulders and cascaded down their backs; black shoes that buckled in the front; and tall, pointed, black hats with wide, round brims. Next to each stood a broom, straw side up. In the entire time Albert had known the witches, this was the first time he had actually seen them dress the part.

"Good morning," said Albert politely, as he nibbled on a piece of the Limburger cheese that had been placed on his spot at the table. "What's with the getups?"

"Oh, they're just for fun," answered Annie, sipping her cup of morning brew. "We only dress this way when we're attending functions, and on Halloween, of course."

Cat, who had been studying a copy of the Witchfest 2,303 schedule, checked her wristwatch. The timepiece was unlike any Albert had ever seen. The watch had no hands. Instead, placed behind a crystal face, were three small hourglasses with grains of sand that seemed to be running a maze.

"It's half past nine. Bailey should be here any minute," announced Cat.

Cat and Annie had asked Bailey to join them for the opening ceremonies of Witchfest. Bailey had confided to them that she was worried that if she sat with her family, she would be seated behind her Aunt Tildy. Not that she didn't love her aunt, she did. It was just that Aunt Tildy's favorite grooming implement was her teasing comb, and as a result, Aunt Tildy had big hair. On more than one occasion, Bailey had had to sit on her knees and crane her neck from side to side to see over the massive beehive hairdo that crowned the top of her aunt's head.

"Albert, you're coming with us to the opening ceremonies, and then you'll be spending the remainder of the day with Eve, Paisley, and the cats," said Catrina, laying the schedule on the table.

When Albert had first heard of this plan it had made him feel more than a little nervous. But Eve and Paisley assured him that cats only ate mice when absolutely necessary, and that all the cats in attendance were very well-cared for and extremely well-fed—information that had eased his mind considerably. He was to make everyone's acquaintance at the cat's banquet, an event he was looking forward to since having been assured he was to be the guest of honor and not an hors d'oeuvre.

"The cats are very interested in meeting a mouse intelligent enough to teach itself to read," purred Eve. "You're a bit famous in our circle."

Albert tried not to let his new celebrity status go to his head, but he couldn't keep from walking a bit taller, and he was finding it quite hard to pass by a mirror without stopping to practice his most serious expressions. To be thought an intellectual by a group of felines was a heady feeling indeed.

Catrina was just about to check her watch again when Bailey arrived.

"Sorry I'm late," said Bailey, as she hurried in from the hallway. "I had a terrible time getting away from mother and Aunt Tildy. They kept fussing over the hem in my cape."

"No problem," said Cat. She reached down, picked up Albert, placed him on the brim of her black pointed hat, and the happy group headed out into the hallway, which was beginning to smell fairly strongly of lavender and jasmine.

"Bailey, would you do the honors?" asked Annie.

"Of course," replied Bailey in her most grown-up voice. She placed her right index finger in front of her and spoke to her directional ring. "To the opening ceremonies of Witchfest 2,303 please," she requested and began leading the way to auditorium A.

The room was already bustling with witches when they arrived. Cat moved Albert to her shoulder, and they all checked their hats and brooms at the door.

"How about those seats?" asked Cat, pointing to three together in the center of the seventh row.

"Looks good to me," said Annie, placing an arm around Bailey's shoulders. "What do you think?"

"Perfect!" replied Bailey.

"Not to be rude," meowed Paisley politely, "but if you don't mind, I think Eve and I are going to join Sebastian in the cat's gallery."

"Not at all. Go right ahead," answered Annie, giving Paisley an affectionate scratch under the chin. "Just remember to meet us in the hallway after the program so you can pick up Albert."

"We'll be there," purred Paisley. And the two cats padded up the stairs to the balcony.

14

Opening Ceremonies

The opening ceremonies were not a disappointment. They got underway by the Scottish witches turning the sconces that lined the walls into dragon's heads that breathed golden flames. This was in addition to the bagpipes they had float through the aisles squeezing out Scottish jigs. Then the group from Australia gave everyone a chance to actually become part of the Great Barrier Reef by conjuring up a hologram that encompassed the auditorium. Not wanting to be outdone, the French transformed the theater into the Louvre, complete with original masterpieces, but not before the Canadians caused maple leaves to sprout from the audience's ears.

Then came the moment Bailey had been waiting for. A voice that came from nowhere yet everywhere rang through the auditorium. "And now, it is with great pleasure that I introduce the High Witch, Hildegard Harrowitz and her lovely Snow Bengal, Charm."

A hush fell over the audience as the lights dimmed, and a spotlight revealed a ring of braided jasmine vines resting in the center of the stage. A white marble pedestal was placed slightly off center within the circle. Silver funnel clouds appeared in the far reaches of the room. Each shone brightly and sparkled with bits of glittering emeralds that seemed to attract what little light there was and reflect it back tenfold.

Wind began blowing from all directions, as the clouds rose and made their way toward the stage. The winds became stronger as the clouds converged in the circle of jasmine and merged into a single tornado, spinning and sparkling exquisitely in the spotlight. The tornado spun faster and faster until, with a loud clap, it vanished and standing in the ring of jasmine was the High Witch herself, Hildegard Harrowitz. Applause broke out as the High Witch, whom Albert could not help but notice looked a bit like Catrina, raised her arms and smiled out at the audience.

Once again, a hush fell over the audience, as more clouds appeared, similar to the first but smaller and glittering with the delicate blue of sapphires. They, too, converged on the stage, merging into a small tornado that balanced itself precariously over the marble pedestal. This tornado, too, spun faster and faster until, with a sharp clap, it vanished, leaving Charm standing majestically in its place. Again applause erupted from the audience, only this time it was accompanied by meows and murmurs from the mezzanine.

"How appropriate for Hildegard to place Charm upon a pedestal," commented a winter-white Persian.

"Yes, yes," agreed an American Shorthair. "After all, isn't that where all cats belong?"

Bailey sat transfixed, staring at the beautifully marked cat standing center stage. Charm wore a collar that consisted of three strands of blue sapphires that were a perfect match for her eyes.

Hildegard had begun to speak, but Bailey had no idea what the High Witch was saying, as she had locked eyes with the beautiful, white cat and fallen completely under her spell. Somehow, she was lost in time and space, as she admired the feline from her place in the seventh row. Albert looked around and noticed that Charm seemed to have this effect on several of the witches in the audience. Then, just as suddenly as Bailey had been taken in, she once again became aware of her surroundings. She shook her head in bewilderment, as she realized Hildegard was concluding her talk.

"So that's our list of activities for the next few days," said the High Witch, smiling at the audience. "On behalf of the Universal Witches Council, I wish you all the very best that magic has to offer."

Hildegard raised her arms and wiggled her fingers. Suddenly, fireworks appeared in the air above the spectators' heads, showering everyone with sparks that turned into small pieces of diamonds, rubies, and emeralds. The gemstones clung to the witches' robes, causing them to shimmer, as the house lights came back up.

"Wow! That was really something!" exclaimed Braden, upon meeting up with his sister in the hallway after the ceremonies let out. He reached out and brushed a ruby from the tip of Bailey's nose.

Bailey looked over at her mother and Aunt Tildy, who were making their way toward her. Bailey wouldn't have believed it possible, but the wind had managed to make Aunt Tildy's hair even bigger.

"Wasn't that just wonderful!" said Tildy.

"Yes, it was," agreed Bailey, hugging her aunt.

"So what are everyone's plans for the rest of the afternoon?" asked Helen Bramblewood. She wanted to make certain her family was properly accounted for prior to going their separate ways.

"Braden and I are going to spend the afternoon in cavern five, where they're demonstrating the latest in flying Volkswagens," answered Basil, placing his hand on his son's shoulder. "And what are you ladies going to be up to?"

"Tildy and I had planned to attend the "Potions to Please" seminar in cavern two, but if I'm not mistaken, Bailey's seminar with Hildegard begins at the same time, and I'm a little concerned about leaving her here on her own."

"You and Aunt Tildy go ahead. I'll be fine," said Bailey, a hint of exasperation in her voice. "I have turned twelve, you know."

"We'll keep an eye on her, Helen," offered Cat. "We're going to be right down the hall cataloging the new spell books that arrived yesterday."

"Thank you," said Helen. She fussed a bit more over the hem in Bailey's cape, kissed her daughter lightly on the top of her head, then scooted off down the hall with Tildy, stopping to smile back at her daughter before turning the corner.

"Sometimes she treats me like such a baby," said Bailey, waving after her mother.

"It's only because she loves you," replied Annie.

"I know," said Bailey, "but she's going to have to let me grow up sometime."

At that moment Eve and Paisley came padding down from the cat's gallery.

"Ready to go, Albert?" purred Eve.

"Ready when you are," answered Albert from his perch on Cat's right shoulder. "Where are we off to, anyway?"

"The Wriggle Room," answered Paisley. "It's scads of fun."

Cat placed Albert gently on Eve's head.

"Now you two look after Albert, and don't let him get lost," directed Annie.

"And Albert, you stay close to Eve and Paisley," commanded Cat.

"Will do," said Albert, saluting, and the three made their way down the hall, Albert riding between Eve's ears.

15

The Wriggle Room

"Welcome to the Wriggle Room," came a voice as
Albert, Eve, and Paisley passed through the door. And
wriggle it did. This was because the entire room was filled
with objects that crept, slithered, squirmed, shimmied,
shot, and quivered. Albert watched in amazement as
shapes of every size, color, and texture imaginable flitted
across the floor, flew through the air, and bounced off the
walls. It was a cat's delight.

"Well, what do you think?" asked Eve, bowing her
head so that Albert could climb off onto the floor.

"I must say," said Albert, looking about, "I've never
seen anything like this."

Albert used the end of his tail to poke at a bright-
orange ball that had begun to circle him. To his surprise
the ball burst, and a soft, cylinder-shaped object sprung
forth and shot toward the ceiling. Paisley made a daring
leap after it. Jumping nearly three feet into the air, she
caught it expertly between her front paws.

"Well done," said Sebastian, who had taken time off from chasing a snake-like object across the middle of the room to join them.

"Thank you," purred Paisley.

"Albert, would you like to join us in pouncing?" asked Eve.

"Actually," said Albert, holding his tail and moving toward the door, "I think I might just watch from a distance." All the cats in the room appeared to be in varied states of frenzy and, although he knew they were all quite friendly, he couldn't help but feel just a tad bit uncomfortable. He stood in the doorway and watched as the cats leaped, pounced, and bounced off the walls and quietly wondered if this was anything like what was happening in Bailey's seminar.

16

Hildegard's Seminar

Bailey was so nervous about meeting Hildegard and Charm in person that she dropped her invitation three times on the way to the lecture hall.

When she arrived, she walked slowly into the room and looked around at the others in attendance. There were witches of different ages, which did not surprise Bailey, as she knew that witches chose to pair with cats at different times for different purposes. What did surprise her was that there was only seating for fifteen. She'd thought a seminar held by Hildegard Harrowitz would have attracted such an audience there would be standing room only.

"Excuse me," said Bailey, addressing a witch who looked to be about her age. "Is this Hildegard Harrowitz's seminar "Pairing with a Cat: What Every Witch Should Know"?

"Yes, it is. Isn't this exciting?" answered the witch enthusiastically. "Hi, I'm Greta Greeley. You must be Bailey Bramblewood. I know because other than myself, you're the only witch attending who's under twenty. You see, I checked out all the statistics on the witches who received invitations. Always good to know who you're keeping company with. You see that male witch over there?" Greta cast a glance at a gentleman who looked to be about thirty. "He's very clever. He's the witch who invented the spell that allows witches to travel through time! Of course, only a few witches have actually accomplished time travel. The spell is quite hard to master, but apparently Malcolm, that's his name, Malcolm Mitchell, can go anywhere in the blink of an eye. It's rumored a Bengal has its eye on him and he wants to make certain that he handles things properly." All this came out in one delightfully long, energetic breath.

"Why so few seats?" questioned Bailey. Somehow, she had the feeling Greta had the scoop on just about everything.

"Oh, didn't you know?" said Greta, looking a little surprised. "This is an invitation-only seminar. There were no outside sign-ups. Every witch here was personally picked by Hildegard Harrowitz herself."

"But I've never met Hildegard," said Bailey, sounding a bit bewildered.

"It doesn't matter. Hildegard wanted you here or you wouldn't have received an invitation, and being here is all that counts. By the way, I've never met her either." Greta looked at Bailey with an expression that said, *I'm as nervous as you are.*

Bailey sat down next to Greta and stared around the room. She wondered if perhaps her invitation had been some sort of mistake.

"No mistake. Your name was definitely on the list." Bailey looked up to find Hildegard staring at her from the doorway. "I know because I put it there myself."

Bailey almost fell off her chair as the High Witch walked toward her.

"You read minds," exhaled Bailey in little more than a whisper.

"Well, you were thinking particularly loudly," answered Hildegard with a wink. "Greta, glad you could make the seminar," she said, turning to the brown-haired, freckled-faced witch sitting next to Bailey.

"You know who I am?" gasped Greta, holding the sides of her chair.

"Of course I know who you are," replied Hildegard, smiling. "You two were my top picks for the seminar. I'm honored you accepted."

"You're honored?" gasped Bailey. "We're the ones who are honored."

"Why, that's the nicest compliment I've had all day," said Hildegard, her bright-green eyes twinkling. "I'm looking forward to getting to know each of you better as the seminar progresses. Now, if you'll excuse me, I have some other guests I should attend to. Charm should be along in a few minutes, and then we'll get started. In the meantime, if you need anything, just let me know."

Bailey and Greta sat staring, eyes big as saucers, as the High Witch walked over to Malcolm, leaned over his shoulder, and whispered something into his ear.

Neither Bailey nor Greta had ever imagined they would actually be able to speak directly to Hildegard and Charm. Both had assumed they would sit through a lecture and, if very lucky, get an opportunity to say hello on the way out. But apparently, this was not what the High Witch had in mind at all. For whatever reasons, she wanted to get to know these witches personally.

As the seminar progressed, Hildegard spent time with each witch. She went over the qualities of each breed of cat, stressing that all cats were equally wonderful. It was just a case of finding one that complemented a witch's particular talents. "Don't be discouraged if you don't find a proper cat right off the bat," said Hildegard. "Remember, cats have to agree to this pairing for a reason. They instinctively know if they are right for you. It's true that you choose your cat, but your cat also chooses you."

Hildegard also encouraged the witches to become acquainted with one another; thus, Bailey was able to learn things about everyone in attendance.

There was Malcolm Mitchell, of course, the great inventor of the time travel spell. Bailey was in awe of him. Transportation spells were the most difficult to perform—so difficult in fact that most witches chose not to fool around with them. It was much easier to enchant a car and shrink it to get to where you wanted to go—and safer, too, since a transportation spell improperly cast could land a witch most anywhere. Bailey couldn't imagine coming up with a spell that not only transported a body from one place to another, but back and forth through time to boot! Malcolm's spell was kept under lock and key. When asked why, he simply answered, "Time is a delicate thing. It's not something you want to go playing around with. Goodness knows what could be altered by even the best-meaning soul."

Bailey found out things about the other witches too. She found out that Greta Greeley had an uncommon ability to pick up languages. While it is true that all witches are able to converse with animals, some animals are much harder to communicate with than others—insects being by far the hardest. There were many witches who never truly mastered beetle, even after years of study. Greta, however, was able to understand and speak fluent beetle by the age of eight months.

One of the top herbalists in the world, Zelda Zimmer, was also in attendance. A petite witch in her mid-sixties, Zelda was responsible for the majority of potions published in the *International Witches Council Book of Plants and Potions*. She was also the former head of the potions department at the Wexford Witching Institute in Scotland.

Bailey liked Zelda immediately. She was fun and full of pep and not at all embarrassed to share both the wonders and the blunders she had been responsible for over the years. "Why, once I accidentally turned all the chairs in one of my first-floor labs into mushrooms when trying out a new herbal mix for cushion softening!" She laughed. "Not only did it take me two weeks to figure out where I had gone wrong, but my students insisted on hopping every time they saw me. Said if they were to be made to sit on toadstools, they may as well act the part. We have a mutual acquaintance, you know," she told Bailey. "Bianca Beechwood, who owns Nature Knows Best in your hometown of Harborville, was one of my best students when I was teaching here in the States. Please send her my regards when you see her next. Tell her Professor Zimmer has not forgotten her. Why, I still have her botany thesis!"

Bailey couldn't help but feel a bit outdone. There was nothing special about her that she should be included among these witches. She had never accomplished anything remarkable. So why had she been asked to attend?

What Bailey did not know, and what Hildegard and Charm did not tell her, was that on the night Bailey was born, seventy-five cats had met to discuss her future and that it was Charm who had specifically asked that Bailey be present at the seminar. When it came to such matters, Hildegard never questioned the wisdom of her cat. Hence, Bailey's name had been placed at the very top of the list.

"OK, Bailey, let's give it a try, shall we?" requested Hildegard, as she held a feather out to her side. The seminar was winding down, and Hildegard was demonstrating the importance of cats in magic. "Remember, the object is to move the feather from my hand to the inside of the sealed jar sitting on the stool."

Bailey, who was experiencing an extreme case of butterflies in her stomach, couldn't believe what she was being asked to do. Having one object move through another was almost as difficult a task as casting a transportation spell. She took a deep breath, raised her hands in front of her, concentrated, and wiggled her fingers at the feather. The feather left Hildegard's hand, picked up speed as it neared the jar, bumped it lightly, and fell to the ground.

"Very good," said Hildegard. "Now try again with Charm's help."

Bailey looked down at Charm, who had come to stand by her side. The young witch's butterflies turned to full-grown bullfrogs as she realized everyone in the room had stopped to watch.

"It's OK," purred Charm. "Just concentrate. I'll be right here."

Hildegard held another feather out to her side, and once again Bailey placed her hands in front of her and wiggled her fingers. This time, the feather sped toward the jar and began butting the glass fiercely with its sharp quill. It circled the jar several times, attempting to pierce the glass from various angles. Bailey took a deep breath and concentrated as hard as she could. Charm, who had been standing with one paw on Bailey's foot, pushed her soft white neck hard against Bailey's shin. To everyone's amazement, the feather backed up three feet, shot straight as an arrow through the jar, and came to rest in the center of the container.

"Well done!" exclaimed Hildegard. "I hope this shows what can be accomplished with the help of a truly great cat. That ends our seminar for today, but I'll be keeping in touch with all of you. Remember, it's important to pair with just the right cat. So, if this Halloween comes and goes without the proper feline making its presence known to you, don't be discouraged. There's always next year. Thank you all for coming."

There was an outbreak of applause, then the witches gathered up their hats and brooms and prepared to leave.

Bailey felt a tap on her shoulder and turned to find Malcolm staring down at her. "You were very good with that feather. I couldn't have done that when I was twelve if I'd had twelve cats helping me."

"Thank you," said Bailey, blushing slightly from the praise. "But I did have Charm helping me. She's a very special cat."

"Yes, she is," agreed Malcolm. "Listen, I spend some time every summer running seminars and lecturing on new spells. Here's my card. If you're interested in attending a class next summer, give me a call. Something tells me you might just have yourself a cat by then." He gave Bailey's hand a light shake, then went off to talk to Hildegard.

Bailey's mouth nearly dropped open as she looked at the card that had been placed in her hand. She placed it carefully into the pocket of her cape, then went in search of Greta. The two witches made plans to meet later that evening. Then Bailey walked out into the hallway where she found Cat and Annie waiting for her.

"Well, how'd it go?" questioned Cat.

"It was remarkable!" exclaimed Bailey. "Hildegard's the best speaker I've ever heard."

"Well, she's one of the best listeners I've ever had," said Hildegard, who had walked up behind Bailey. "Cat, Annie, it's good to see you. How are things at the library?"

"Quite well, thank you," answered Cat. "And how are things with you? I got your note last week. Did Cousin Mildred enjoy her trip to Spain?"

Bailey was a bit confused. She didn't know the two witches even knew each other, yet here they were, exchanging information about a family member who had gone off on holiday.

"Hildegard and I are cousins," Cat informed Bailey. "We grew up three blocks from each other."

Bailey looked closely at the two cousins. Hildegard was taller than Cat and had long, mahogany-colored hair that she wore swept into a French twist, but there was no mistaking the family resemblance. The bright-green eyes, delicate noses, and high cheekbones were nearly identical. Bailey couldn't believe she had not noticed it before.

"Where are you off to now?" asked Hildegard.

"We're going to meet Eve and Paisley so we can pick up Albert," replied Cat.

"Oh, the reading mouse you brought along." Hildegard grinned. "Mind if I tag along? I've been wanting to meet the little rascal."

Cat checked her directional ring, and the small group made their way toward the Wriggle Room. When they arrived, they found Eve and Paisley waiting for them outside the door.

"We have a problem," said Eve sheepishly. "We seem to have lost Albert."

"What do you mean, you lost him?" questioned Cat, looking down at Eve and Paisley. "I thought you two promised to keep an eye on him."

"We're so sorry," meowed Eve. "We asked him to join us in pouncing, but he declined and told us he'd wait by the door. The next thing we knew, he was gone. Oh, if anything happens to him, we'll never forgive ourselves."

Normally, Cat and Annie would have lectured the two cats for being so irresponsible, but the two felines were so upset about losing Albert, it seemed cruel to punish them further.

"Don't worry," said Hildegard, staring down at the cats. "The caverns are deep, but there isn't much mischief for your friend to get into. Why don't you two go back to your room in case he shows up there, and we'll check the rest of the caverns. He couldn't have gone far."

17

Lost in the Caverns of Hanhoo

Albert sat down and clutched his tail tightly between his paws. He hadn't meant to get lost. He just wanted to take a little look around. He had carefully counted the turns so that he could find his way back, but somehow he had become confused and had managed to wander deeper and deeper into the caverns.

He looked around for a place to rest, but nothing looked inviting. He had been walking for what seemed an eternity and had ended up in a place that was damp and dreary. And as if this were not bad enough, it was beginning to get dark. *At least I got away from that terrible smell*, he thought to himself. Earlier, he had turned down one passage that had smelled strongly of rotten fish, though how a fish could have found its way into the caverns was beyond him.

He took a breath and trudged on, one paw holding his tail, the other tugging at his whiskers. He saw an opening for a chamber and crept inside. Looking about, he found a mouse-size crevice along one of the walls. He scaled the rock and squeezed in, hoping he had found a safe place to rest. He carefully surveyed the chamber from his place in the crevice. With the exception of some stalactites and stalagmites, and a crack in the rock ceiling that was just large enough to show a darkening sky, the chamber looked like all the others he had stumbled in and out of.

Albert was just about to close his eyes when he caught a glimpse of something directly across from him. There, hanging onto the wall as if for dear life, was a vine with small, oval leaves and a delicate, white bud. Albert watched as the plant turned and began stretching its long, thin stem upward along the side of the cavern. It snaked its way silently up the rock wall until it was only a few inches from the crack in the ceiling. It then came to a halt and turned its bud back down toward the small mouse who lay curled up in the crevice.

For one fleeting moment, Albert thought of the evil vine that occupied Miss Prattle's office and wondered if perhaps he should find another spot to rest. But this plant wasn't frightening at all. Somehow, it seemed kind and precious—not at all like the nightmare that had rooted itself in the library. Suddenly, Albert felt a warm welcome feeling wash over him, as if the plant were glad for the company. And perhaps it was, because after Albert had fallen asleep, and the moonlight washed through the crack in the ceiling, it raised its stem toward the warm night sky and bloomed.

18

Irwin

"Well, where shall we start?" asked Cat, looking around her. The caverns were connected by a maze of tunnels, and the witches had no idea which direction Albert had started off in.

"How about that way?" said Annie, pointing toward a long tunnel to her left.

"It's as good a place as any," answered Hildegard, and the group set off.

They hadn't walked far before Bailey had an idea. "Can't we just ask our directional rings to take us to Albert?"

"I'm afraid that wouldn't work," answered Hildegard. "You see, Albert wasn't here and in place when the ring spell was cast on the caverns, so it won't locate him. But don't worry, we'll find him."

They continued on, and Bailey noticed that the farther they went, the more twists and turns the tunnels took. The passages forked off in all directions, and it was easy to see how a body could become lost.

They walked on, stopping occasionally to call out Albert's name. After a while they turned down a particularly narrow, twisty tunnel and were suddenly met by the smell of rotten fish.

"Yuck!" gasped Bailey, holding her nose. "What's that smell?"

"That," Hildegard said, turning her head slightly to one side, "would be Irwin."

Irwin was a genie who had taken up residence in the Caverns of Hanhoo. He, like most genies, was large and formidable looking; however, unlike other genies, he refused to call anyone "master." Nor did he make his home in a lamp or bottle but instead chose to reside in a large, stuffed fish, which he had mounted on the wall of one of the tunnels. The fish itself had lost its odor years ago, but Irwin had wished a spell on it causing it to reek so badly that no one would come close, least yet disturb him. He was, to put it politely, a wee bit grumpy.

Irwin was also very lazy. It was rumored that he had once slept for thirty-seven years but had decided never to do this again, as it was far too long to go without lunch and a good cup of tea. He now limited his naps to no more than twelve days, lest his stomach should begin to rumble.

"Irwin," called Hildegard, tapping the stuffed fish on its side, "are you in there?"

"Go away!" rumbled a voice from deep inside the fish.

"Irwin, you come out of there right now, or I'll seal up your fish and throw you into the ocean."

"Who dares disturb me?" bellowed the deep voice.

The tunnel shook slightly, and black smoke began to billow from the fish's mouth. It gathered into a dark cloud that took the shape of a large man who stood suspended before the small search party, his feet threaded into the opening from which he had emerged.

"Oh, Hildegard, it's you," said the genie, staring down at the group of witches below. His manners improved a bit once he realized he was in the presence of the High Witch. "What do you desire of me?"

"For starters, you could do away with the smell," said Hildegard, looking sternly into the genie's eyes.

"Done," said Irwin, crossing his arms against his massive chest. "Now, why have you disturbed my slumber?"

"We're looking for a mouse," said Hildegard. "Small, brown, long tail."

"I know what a mouse looks like," roared Irwin, raising his eyebrows.

"Good, then you'll have no trouble directing us to him," smiled back Hildegard.

"You mean to tell me you woke me to help you find a misplaced mouse?" bellowed Irwin.

"Yes, I did, and you'll watch yourself, or you'll suffer the same fate as Kazmar," said Hildegard, taking a step toward the angry genie.

To Bailey's amazement Irwin backed down immediately.

"No harm meant, really, Hildegard," said the genie, lowering his voice and taking on a less menacing demeanor. "No need for threats. I've seen the mouse you speak of. Take the third tunnel to your left, then a quick right. You should find him sleeping in a crevice in one of the caverns. He stumbled through about an hour ago. Now, with your permission, I'll return to my nap."

"Thank you, Irwin," said Hildegard politely. And they all watched as the genie turned back into smoke and was inhaled by the fish.

"Who's Kazmar?" asked Bailey, looking a bit pale. She had never met a genie before, and the encounter had left her a bit shaken.

"Kazmar was a very bad genie," answered Hildegard.

"Worse than that one?" asked Bailey, looking back to where the fish hung mounted against the wall.

"Much worse," answered Hildegard. "He had it in for anyone or anything that wasn't a genie. He was determined to rid the world of witches and mortals and probably would have succeeded if he hadn't been stopped."

"How did you stop him?" asked Bailey. She felt her stomach begin to tie up in knots.

"About three hundred years ago, the Scottish witches ganged up on him," answered Hildegard. "They hit him with every spell they could come up with. They finally managed to rob him of most of his powers and place them in his lamp. Then they buried the lamp," answered Hildegard, as the group traipsed deeper into the caverns.

"Where is it buried?" asked Bailey.

"No one knows. There was only one map that showed its location, and it was thrown into the sea years ago, so the lamp's whereabouts could not be revealed."

"So what happened to Kazmar?"

"Oh, he's still around," answered Hildegard. "But I don't think you need to concern yourself with him. He has very little power now and can't hurt anyone. He's really rather pathetic."

Bailey felt relief wash over her. She was glad to hear that the genie had been stopped. The whole event sounded like a tale made up to frighten children.

"Well, look what we have here," whispered Hildegard, looking into the entrance of one of the caverns.

There, lying curled up in a small ball in a crevice, was Albert, fast asleep and snoring contently.

19

Return to a Troubled Town

Albert was thankful to have been found, and he did not stray off on his own for the remainder of his stay in the caverns. Instead, he watched safely from the brim of Bailey's hat as she and Greta attended the "Silly Spells" workshop and sat quietly on Basil Bramblewood's wide shoulder as he and Braden attended yet another flying Volkswagen demonstration. On their last night in the caverns—since the others had had the good taste and manners not to mention his little misadventure to anyone—he took center stage at the cat's banquet, where he dazzled everyone with his knowledge of Shakespeare and Keats.

Then, as all vacations must end, it was time to go home. Bailey and Greta promised to keep in touch and report to each other on their progress in pairing with a proper cat. And, after many farewells, the Witchfest-goers began to depart.

Albert waved good-bye to everyone from his perch on Cat's shoulder, as his small group followed the Bramblewoods out to the parking lot. Cat and Annie happily noted that Mr. Bramblewood was wearing a broad smile and jingling the keys to a new Volkswagen.

As luck would have it, it was a glorious day to be flying. Cat and Annie opened the windows and allowed the warm summer air to flow through the car, while Albert lay lazily upon the dashboard composing the stories he would tell his cousins. He could imagine the looks on their faces as he relayed how he, cousin Albert, had sat casually conversing at a banquet table full of cats. He could see their eyes widen as he told them how he had met the High Witch, Hildegard Harrowitz, and recounted the events of the opening ceremonies. And he could hear them gasp as he told them about the Wriggle Room, and how he had stood bravely in the midst of frenzied felines and stabbed one of the wiggling objects with his tail. He decided he would leave out the part about how he had become lost and frightened. After all, he reasoned, why bore everyone with nonessential details?

Albert had just finished putting together his last story when Annie banked the car to the left and sailed it through the crack in the corner of her garage, bringing it to a gentle rest in the middle of the room.

Again Albert felt a strange sensation in his stomach as he was returned to normal size, then everyone piled out of the car, glad for the trip but happy to be home.

Cat and Annie pulled the black spots off the VW Beetle and stowed them in the trunk while Eve and Paisley went off to find their friends. Albert waited for the witches to finish, then the three started off to the library to return Albert to his cigar box and check on the repairs to the building.

They chatted happily as they made their way down the street, but their smiles soon turned to frowns as they heard the distant sounds of doors slamming and people raising their voices in anger.

They became even more concerned as they approached the library, for there, sitting on the building's stairs, ears down and tail wrapped tightly around his body, was the McFarlands' collie, Andrew.

"Something's wrong," said Andrew, looking up at the witches with mournful brown eyes. "Something is wrong with the people of Harborville."

Catrina stooped down and stroked the collie's head. "What do you mean, something's wrong? Andrew, would this have anything to do with the fact that the library is in worse shape than when we left?"

Cat could not help but notice that the repairs to the building appeared to have come to a halt mid-job. Shingles had been torn off but not replaced, and rolls of tarpaper and loose nails littered the library's roof. Paint cans and brushes had been left under the windows' wooden frames, along with a roll of masking tape and a large brown tarp. It looked as if the workers had just walked away.

"I think," said Andrew, looking around him, "that this is where it started."

"Where what started?" asked Cat

"It's hard to explain," said Andrew, shaking his head so that his white ruff rippled out in all directions. "It's like everyone's mad about something. I'd try to explain it to you, but I think you had best talk to Carl and

Bianca. They sent me here to wait for you. They want you and Annie to meet them at Bianca's shop. They said you should hurry."

Cat put a protective hand over Albert, who sat listening from her shoulder. As the group headed for Nature Knows Best, Albert sat quietly, thinking about the plant that was growing inside the library. As they turned the corner, he looked back at the brick building and what he saw made his whiskers quiver. Standing at a second-story window was the sharp-featured director. Albert watched as she took a pinch of powder from a jar, placed it in the palm of her hand, and blew it out into the warm summer wind.

Once again, Albert felt a strange sensation stir within his stomach, but this time it had nothing to do with a shrinking spell.

20

An Angry Town

When the group arrived at Nature Knows Best, they found Carl and Bianca in the corner of the greenhouse that housed Bianca's desk and bookshelves. They were calling off titles to Emily, who was busily running along the top shelf locating the books.

"Albert," squeaked Emily, as she saw her brother enter the room. "You're back!"

"Are we glad to see you," said Carl, as Cat and Annie approached the desk. "We seem to be having a little problem here."

"So we hear," said Annie. "Andrew met us at the library and said we should come straight away."

"Good boy, Andrew," said Carl, reaching down and patting the dog on his head. "We can always count on you."

"Carl, what is going on?" questioned Cat, more puzzled than ever.

"Better start from the beginning, Carl," said Bianca, looking up from where she was seated behind her desk.

"Well," said Carl. "The day after you left for Witchfest, the crew showed up to start work on the library. They all seemed in good spirits, sharing jokes and coffee and the like. But about an hour into the job, they began to argue with one another. Sam Paulson accused Roy McAfee of using his hammer without asking, and Adam Jolson began barking out orders like a drill sergeant readying recruits. By noon they were all so angry with one another that they up and walked off the job. Just dropped everything and left. Everyone chalked it up to a labor dispute and figured it would eventually work itself out, but then other things began happening. Mrs. Wilkerson accused Mrs. Catalano of not pruning her tulip poplars properly and threatened to cut off the branches that hang over in her yard, and the sparrows that frequent the Lawson's bird feeders complained to Merris that the family was quarreling so badly that they had forgotten to fill the feeder cups. Still," said Carl "we chalked it up to tempers flaring with the summer heat. At least we did until the incident with Ellie Goodman."

"What happened with Ellie?" asked Annie

"Well," said Carl, looking down at the collie that sat droop eared at his feet. "Andrew was at his post at the corner crosswalk when a group of youngsters came by. Only they weren't behaving themselves as they usually do. They were pushing and shoving, and Ellie, as usual, stepped out of the crosswalk. So of course Andrew, being the diligent dog that he is, gently nudged her back in. But instead of Ellie throwing her arms around his neck and giving him a hug as she always does, she pushed him away and yelled at him."

"She called me," said Andrew, dropping his chin so low it nearly met with the floor, "bad dog".

Cat looked down at the dog whose head was hung low in shame. She knew something had to be terribly wrong for sweet little Ellie to treat Andrew so badly.

"Since then, things have gotten worse," continued Carl. "People who have lived peaceably side by side for years are bickering about everything from property lines to crabgrass. The sanitation department, along with just about everyone else who does business with the town, is disputing its contracts, and the mayor refuses to give an inch. He got so mad yesterday, he called off the Founders' Day celebration, which may not be such a bad thing, considering what this place is going to smell like if they don't negotiate another trash pickup sometime soon. Nearly everyone in town seems to be mad about something. The only ones not affected are the witching population and the animals." Carl stopped long enough to gently brush at a flibat that had landed on his bulbous nose. The flibat buzzed and circled his head once before coming to rest on his large glasses, where it hung upside down from their lower rim. "And, as if all of this weren't confusing enough," he continued, "two days ago this arrived."

Carl pointed to the latest edition of the *Witch's Weekly News* that lay spread open on Bianca's desk. The front page bore the headline "**Missing Witch: Community Seeks Help in Solving the Disappearance of Loved Teacher.**" Below was a picture of a black-haired witch with dancing, dark eyes and a sweet smile.

Albert stared at the picture. There was something oddly familiar about the face, but he couldn't quite place it.

"Sharpen the features," directed Bianca, as everyone focused on the photograph.

"It can't be!" exclaimed Annie, taking a closer look.

"But it is," said Carl, concern in his voice. "It's Miss Prattle."

Cat read the newspaper article out loud:

Your help is asked in locating a missing witch. Prudence Prattle disappeared in the Scottish Highlands in August of last year. She was visiting the area in an attempt to collect rare plant specimens to share with her students at the Wexford Witching Institute. At first it was thought that the dedicated teacher had prolonged her stay to further study plant life indigenous to the area; however, when she failed to return after the beginning of the term last fall, authorities became suspicious. Prudence is one of the institute's most loved and respected teachers. Her gentle manner and caring ways have endeared her to students and staff alike. If anyone has any information with regard to her whereabouts, they are requested to contact the Wexford Witching Institute immediately.

"That description," said Albert, narrowing his eyes to mere slits, "hardly fits the dragon lady who dwells in our library."

"Well, she's obviously not well," said Carl, casting a glance at Albert. "And don't speak ill of dragons."

"I totally agree with you," said Cat, sounding perplexed. "Someone or some *thing* has done something to her."

"I contacted the Wexford Institute," said Bianca. "They're sending a Mr. Amos to help. He's completed advanced studies in botany and potions and was working with Miss Prattle up until her disappearance last fall. The institute said he should be arriving sometime tomorrow. I'm not sure of the exact time; the connection was very poor. In the meantime they've asked that we keep track of Prudence's whereabouts but that we not attempt to approach her. They were very adamant that we keep our distance. Andrew, do you think you could keep guard and let us know if she goes anywhere?"

"I'm on it!" said Andrew, rising and heading toward the door. Albert was glad to note that there was a renewed spring in the collie's step as he trotted off to fulfill his duty.

"Albert, you had better stay here near your family. I don't want you back in the library until we've straightened all this out," said Cat.

"If you like, I'll conjure up a crate for you so you'll have your own place," offered Bianca. "I know once you've been on your own, it can be hard to share your space."

"That's very kind of you," said Albert. "As much as I love my family, it would be a bit hard to move back home." Albert tugged at his tail. He was glad for his own place, but he had to admit to himself that there was a certain comfort in being close to his family.

"Has anyone heard from Wanda?" questioned Cat. "She and Gladys are due back from the beach today. I really don't like the thought of them being exposed to whatever the townspeople are suffering from."

"Ummm, you don't have to worry about that," said Carl, looking down at the tips of his shoes. "I sent Wanda and Gladys a box of chocolates laced with a stay-put potion. Wanda called yesterday—seems the two have decided to extend their stay by a week."

"Good thinking, Carl," said Annie.

"Well, since there's nothing more to be done until Mr. Amos arrives, I think we should all go home and get a good night's sleep," suggested Carl. "Something tells me we're going to need it. What do you say we meet back here at nine o'clock tomorrow morning?"

Everyone nodded in agreement.

Albert stopped in to see his parents and say goodnight to his siblings before heading off to the crate that had been conjured for him next to the sage bushes. Once settled into his temporary home, he lay on his back, looking out his window and on through the greenhouse glass at the stars shining above. He wished he could read himself to sleep, but his book-shrinking glasses were still in the library, tucked safely in the hem of the blue cotton curtains where he had stowed them for safekeeping.

Tomorrow's going to be a long day, he thought as he pulled the covers up over his matchbox bed. *A long day, indeed.*

21

The New Arrival

For the second time in a week, Albert woke to find himself wrapped mummy-style in his sheets with a nightmare about Miss Prattle's plant fresh in his memory. Only this time, not only were the vines reaching for him and wrapping him tightly in their green grasp, but the black-tipped tendrils bore fangs and snapped at him. The more he struggled, the tighter the grip and the closer the fangs.

Albert untangled himself from his bed sheets and ran to the door. He wanted to make certain the plant had not shown up on his doorstep sometime in the night. *Get a grip,* he told himself, as he looked out into the calm of the greenhouse.

A quick glance at the clock told him that it was not quite 6:00 a.m., yet Bianca was up and working at her desk, Emily by her side. The two had their heads together, searching the pages of a large, black book while nibbling on their breakfast.

"Good morning," said Albert, scurrying up the leg of the desk. "What are you two up to?"

"We're gathering material for Mr. Amos to use," answered Bianca, popping a piece of popover in her mouth and washing it down with a sip of herbal tea. "There's fresh cheese and sunflower seeds if you're hungry." She pointed to a small, silver tray sitting next to a glass paperweight. "And what are you doing up so early?"

"Couldn't sleep," said Albert. He did not volunteer that this was due to nightmares about mouse-eating plants.

"A lot of that going around," said Bianca. "Cat and Annie have already called this morning. They're on their way over now."

Bianca had barely finished her sentence when the greenhouse door opened, and Cat and Annie walked in, accompanied by Bailey.

"Look who we found out on the street this time of the morning," said Cat, patting Bailey on the head. "Merris met the Bramblewoods last night when they got home and filled them in on the situation here. Basil and Braden are with Carl. They're hoping to keep the arguing in the community to a minimum, and Bailey here has kindly offered to help us in any way she can."

"Why, thank you, Bailey," said Bianca. "Something tells me we're going to need all the help we can get. Emily and I have been searching through some of my books, and from what we can tell, the sharp features and bad temper Miss Prattle is displaying are indicative of a plant potion. It is our opinion that Miss Prattle has been poisoned."

"You mean," said Albert looking down at the soft, smiling woman who stared back at him from the front of the *Witch's Weekly News*, "that the Miss Prattle we know is the product of a poisonous potion?"

"That's exactly what I mean," said Bianca, thumbing through the large, black book she and Emily had been browsing. "According to the *Encyclopedia of Potions*, plant potions are more effective than spells when it comes to altering a witch's features and personality."

"And what about the townspeople? Any hint as to what's wrong with them?" asked Cat.

"Not yet. Hopefully, Mr. Amos will have some idea when he arrives."

Cat was about to ask Bianca if she had heard anything more about Mr. Amos's arrival time when there was a knock at the shop's front door.

"A bit early for customers, isn't it?" asked Annie.

"One would think so," said Bianca, rising and heading for the greenhouse door. She made her way through to the front shop and returned a short time later carrying a large box wrapped neatly in brown paper.

The parcel, tied with thin jute, was marked Fragile—This End Up, Handle with the Utmost Care! Extremely Precious Cargo!

"Well, this is certainly curious," said Cat, examining the package. "It's from the Wexford Institute."

Bianca carefully placed the package on her desk and snipped at the jute with her pruning shears. With great care, she removed the brown paper and tore down the sides of the box to expose a dollhouse-size replica of a country cottage, complete with detailed trim and thatched roof.

The group stood and watched as the front door opened, and the most beautiful mouse Albert had ever seen stepped out to greet them. She had rich, chestnut-brown fur with a white diamond crest just beneath her throat and thin, round ears. Her tail was long and slim and smooth. And her eyes…*Well*, thought Albert, *those are eyes a mouse could get lost in.*

The delicate, little mouse looked up through long, dark lashes and squeaked in a sweet Scottish accent, "Ye look a wee bit surprised to see me. Didna the institute tell ye I was coming?"

"Oh, yes," said Bianca, as the rest looked on, speechless. "It's just that when they phoned, they said they were sending a Mr. Amos."

"You didna hear corrrrrectly," replied the new arrival. "It's not Mr. Amos, it's Miss A. Mouse. Miss Ailie Mouse, to be more precise, here to help you with your dilemma."

"Well, where are our manners?" said Catrina, finding her voice. She extended her pinky finger for Ailie to shake. "I'm Catrina Cantwick, this is Annie Arkinson, Bianca Beechwood here is with whom you'll be working, this young lady is Bailey Bramblewood, and this is Albert and his sister Emily."

Albert did not know what had come over him. His whiskers were twitching, and his knees felt weak. He stood staring at Ailie while sporting a silly grin.

"It's nice to meet all of you," replied Ailie politely.

She looked up at Albert with her large, brown eyes. "Albert, Hildegard came to see me before I left. She told me she met you at Witchfest. It seems as though we have a bit in common. My cottage usually resides in the academic library adjacent to the institute. It appears we are both very interested in books."

Albert wanted desperately to say something witty and smart, but his speech failed him. All he could do was stand moon-eyed and stare.

"You alrrrrright there, Albert? You seem a bit green. This epidemic your townspeople are suffering from, has it spread to the animal population?"

"No, no. We animals are fine," piped up Emily, who was finding her brother's speechless state more than a little amusing.

"It's very nice to meet you," squeaked Albert, in a voice that did not sound his own.

Emily looked at her brother, who stood staring starry-eyed at Ailie, and an impish grin began to form on her face. "Don't know what's come over him," said Emily. "He's usually a little more chatty. As a matter of fact, we generally have a terrible time shutting him up."

"That's enough, Emily," said Albert, placing a paw on his sister's shoulder.

"If Mom has said it once, she's said it a thousand times; the one thing she'd never have to worry about was Albert ever running out of things to say."

"Emily, dear, don't you think you should run along home?" muttered Albert, through gritted teeth.

"I *am* home. You're the one who's in temporary housing, remember? You'll have to forgive him, Ailie," continued Emily. "For some reason he just doesn't seem to be himself today. Albert, you're not feeling moonstruck, are you?"

Albert slapped a paw over Emily's mouth and nodded toward Ailie. "Younger sibling, you know how it is."

"Oh, I should think so," said Ailie, giving Albert the sweetest smile he had ever seen. "I myself am the oldest of twenty-two."

"So how do you know Prudence?" asked Catrina.

"Prudence and I are both friends and colleagues," said Ailie. "It was Prudence who got me started at the institute. She's a dear, that one."

"I'm afraid you may be in for a bit of a shock when you meet up with her," warned Cat. "She's fallen victim to a poisonous potion that has not only caused a change to her physical appearance, but to her personality as well. She's not exactly what one would consider "warm and fuzzy" at the moment.

"I understand that," said Ailie sadly. "But it's imporrrrtant you remember that she hasn't always been this way. The Prudence I know is as tender a dear girl as you'd ever have the pleasure to meet, and hopefully she will be again after we come up with an antidote. Then," she said, her voice changing from one of sadness and concern to one of pure determination, "I intend to find out just who it is that's responsible for all of this."

Albert looked at the determined little mouse standing outside her cottage door. He remembered reading somewhere that the name Ailie was Gaelic and meant *noble*.

Ailie, thought Albert, *suits her*.

22

Wind Gusts and Weather Vanes

Ailie and Bianca wasted no time in getting to work. Within an hour many of the books from Bianca's bookcase lay spread open around the greenhouse, and the list of the plants that could have been used to produce Prudence Prattle's symptoms had been narrowed to about a dozen, all of which were in the nightshade family.

"We seem to be closing in on Prudence's problem, but we're no closer to figuring out what's going on with the townspeople," sighed Bianca. "I have absolutely no idea what could be causing them to be so irritated with one another."

"It would certainly help to know how they were exposed to whatever it is that is having this ill effect on them," said Ailie, rubbing a delicate paw across her forehead.

As luck would have it, Eve and Paisley picked just that moment to come padding into the room.

"Where have you two been pussyfooting around?" asked Cat, as the two felines jumped up onto the desk and began inspecting Ailie's cottage.

"We've been out interviewing the cats in the area to see if they know anything about what's going on," answered Eve, eyeing the small house with great interest. "Where did this come from?"

"Scotland, as did I," came a reply from the opposite end of the desk.

"And who, may I ask, are you?"

"I'm Ailie. And you two must be Eve and Paisley. Hildegard has told me a lot about you. It's verrrry nice to make your acquaintance."

Albert noticed that Ailie did not seem in the least bit nervous about being in the presence of strange cats. She even walked over to Eve, where she dared to stand next to one of the tabby's sharp-clawed paws.

"It's very nice to meet you, Ailie," purred Eve. "Are you here from the Wexford Institute?"

"Why, yes, I am. Now how did you know that?"

"News travels fast in our circle," replied Eve. "As I said before, Paisley and I spent the entire night out talking to other cats in the area, and I think we've discovered something that might be of interest to you. It seems that all of the fighting started on the north side of town, and according to Celine, the gray tabby that lives down the street, there was a northerly breeze blowing that day. She also informed me that the following day, the bickering spread to the northeast at just about the same time Mrs. Abershire's weather vane picked up enough of a wind gust to move its arrow in that very same direction."

Ailie gave Eve a nod and patted her soft, orange paw. "That, my dearrrr," she said, "is most helpful indeed."

"Well, if you'll excuse us now," said Eve, placing her front paws out in front of her and bowing her back into a good stretch. "We're off to nap. All that running around last night has left us a bit tired."

The two cats circled the greenhouse looking for a proper place to snooze. They passed the catnip bed, knowing it would tempt them to play instead of rest, and opted instead to snuggle among the newly sprouted lavender. The calming scent of lavender, mixed with the warm golden light that streamed in through the greenhouse windows, worked its magic, and both cats soon fell into a deep and welcome sleep.

Bailey, who had been helping pull books from a shelf, could not help but overhear the conversation. "What has Mrs. Abershire's weather vane got to do with any of this?" she asked.

"Well," said Bianca, "it's quite possible that whatever it is that's causing the townspeople to become so angry is being carried by the wind. The problem is we still have to figure out exactly what it is and how it's finding its way into the breeze."

"I think," said Albert, giving his whiskers a dignified pull and trying his best to sound scholarly in front of Ailie, "that I have the answers to those questions."

Albert had indeed caught Ailie's attention, but any thoughts he had of making a good impression on the small Scottish mouse went out the window, as he realized that he would now have to explain how he knew about Miss Prattle's plant.

With all eyes on him, Albert launched into his story. He told how he had made his way up to Miss Prattle's office and run under the door to escape the exterminators and how he had come face-to-leaf with the massive plant that occupied the room. He told them how the entire thing sprouted from a thimble-size pot and how further visits to the office had found Miss Prattle grinding the leaves into powder and storing it in a jar. He then told them how he had seen the director standing in the second-story window blowing the contents of the jar out into the warm summer wind. He left out the part about how the plant had given him nightmares as it just seemed too unmousely a thing to share in front of Ailie.

"I'm sorry I didn't mention any of this sooner," apologized Albert, "but I didn't make the connection until now."

"No need to apologize," said Cat. "How were you to know the plant was anything more than what it appeared?"

"Albert," said Ailie, "do you think if you saw a picture of this plant, you would recognize it?"

"Absolutely," said Albert thinking it couldn't possibly resemble any other plant. Besides, he wanted desperately to help, for even though he knew no one blamed him for not coming forward with the information sooner, he felt a bit guilty. After all, if he had told someone earlier, perhaps the townspeople could have been spared all their arguing, and Harborville would still be a peaceful, happy town.

Ailie showed Albert pictures of several plants. To Albert's amazement, they all looked very similar to the plant in Miss Prattle's office. All were large and leafy, sprung from small beginnings, and bloomed in colors of orange, purple, and yellow.

"I think," said Albert, pointing to one of the pictures, "that it's this one, but I'm not entirely sure. They all look alike."

"I know," said Ailie with some concern. "They're almost impossible to tell apart unless you have a leaf in front of you, which of course we don't. Unfortunately, in order for us to produce a cure for the townspeople, we're going to have to know which variety Prudence used to make them behave the way they are. I know it's an awfully bad position to put you in, Albert, but could you please just give it your best guess?"

"I'll do better than that," said Albert, thinking he may have found a way to redeem himself and impress Ailie. "I'll bring you a leaf from the plant."

23

A Potion for Prudence

"Alberrrt, dearrr," said Ailie, eyeing her new acquaintance with some concern, "the only way for you to get a piece of that plant is to go back into the library, which is very brave but not very practical. I've been told that, in her current state, Prudence does not care much for mice who are not causing trouble. I cannot imagine what she would do to one she caught trying to tear a piece from her plant."

"I know it's dangerous," said Albert, lowering his voice and standing as tall as a two-inch mouse could stand. "But someone has to take on this mission, and I'm the only mouse for the job."

"Oh, pleeease," said Emily under her breath.

"You know, Albert might be right," said Bianca. "Ailie and I have found a universal potion that should act as an antidote for any plant-based poison that is in the nightshade family, so it should work on Prudence. Why don't you wait until we concoct the antidote, then Cat and

Annie and I, will take it to the library. We'll find Prudence and get her to drink the potion. While she's distracted, Albert can tear off a leaf and bring it back here for Ailie to study. That way, Ailie will know exactly what it is that Prudence has been growing and can start to work on a cure for the town."

"Good thinking," said Cat, turning to Bianca. "Only Annie and I can handle getting the potion into Prudence by ourselves. You should stay here and help Ailie identify the plant."

"Actually, it's best if I go along," replied Bianca. "Prudence is probably not going to take the potion willingly, and you may need an extra hand. Besides, she could have an odd reaction to the antidote and need my care. One can't be too careful."

"You're right there," said Ailie. "Any number of strrrrange things could occur. And it's best you remember that in her present state, Prudence may be trickier than you think. It's a good plan, but not without its risks. You'd best be prepared for anything and everything."

Ailie and Bianca immediately set to work on the antidote for Prudence. Emily and Bailey pitched in by collecting needed items, and thanks to the well-orchestrated efforts of the group, the potion was finished within the hour.

"Well, here it is," said Ailie, resting her paw against a vial of blue-green liquid. "Make certain she drinks it all, as half a dose simply wouldn't be enough."

"We'll get it all down her, Ailie," said Bianca. "Well, ladies and gentleman, are you ready?"

"Absolutely," answered Annie.

"Bailey, would you mind waiting here until we get back?" asked Bianca. "We may need your help with the cure for the townspeople."

"No problem," replied Bailey.

Cat picked up Albert and placed him on her shoulder.

"Be careful, Albert," called Emily, as a wave or apprehension swept over her.

"He'll be fine," said Ailie, trying her best to sound confident. She placed a comforting paw on Emily's shoulder. "They'll all be just fine, you'll see."

24

Vengeful Vines

Cat checked to make certain Albert had a secure perch on her shoulder then she, Annie, and Bianca stepped out into the midmorning sun and looked around them. Since all the townspeople were too busy bickering to open any of the businesses, the streets were deserted. The only one to be found was Andrew, who stood diligently guarding his post in front of the library. As the four approached, the collie trotted up to them.

"Is she still in there?" asked Cat.

"No one has come in or out since I've been here," answered Andrew. "There have, however, been some strange sounds coming from the basement."

"What kind of sounds?" asked Annie.

"Thudding noises," answered Andrew. "Do you want me to continue to keep watch?"

"No, thank you, Andrew," said Cat. "We're here now, and the McFarlands are probably wondering where you've strayed off to. I think it's best if you check in so they don't think you've gone missing."

"You're probably right," said Andrew. "They do tend to worry about me. Besides, I need to check on them. Hopefully they're not arguing with each other. They're such a kind couple. It breaks my heart to think they could have fallen victim to whatever this is that's going around. If you need anything, send someone to find me." The collie turned and trotted off in the direction of his home.

As the group prepared to enter the library, they heard the thudding noises Andrew had mentioned. A look through the basement window revealed their source which, oddly enough, turned out to be Miss Prattle and a tall, thin man in an overcoat. The two were hacking away at the basement floor with a pickax and a shovel. Lying near them, brittle and yellowed, was an old parchment map with an *X* marked in the lower left-hand corner.

"What on earth is she doing?" questioned Cat, as she moved away from the window so as not to be seen.

"She appears to be digging," answered Annie.

"Who's that with her?" asked Bianca.

"I've no idea," replied Cat. "Annie, how about you?"

"Not a clue," answered Annie.

"How are we going to get Prudence alone?" asked Bianca. "It's going to be hard enough to force this antidote down her throat. The last thing we need is an audience."

"I quite agree," answered Cat. She thought for a minute then said. "Let's try this. When we get inside, Albert, you run up to the office and tear off a piece of the plant to take back to Ailie. Annie and I will call down to Prudence and tell her we have some library business. Bianca, you wait by the circulation desk. Hopefully, whoever is down there with her won't follow her up the stairs, and we can corner her and try to administer the antidote."

"Sounds like a plan to me," said Annie.

The group trooped up the back stairs, through the lobby, and entered the children's library. Cat placed Albert on the floor so he could take off to the director's office, while the others positioned themselves and readied to call down for Miss Prattle.

Albert ran over to the children's corner and quickly scaled the blue cotton curtains. He was just about to squeeze through the wall vent when he heard a rustling noise below him. Albert looked down just in time to see large, snakelike vines slither out from behind the stacks and coil around his friends. The three witches struggled with all their might but could not free themselves. They pulled and tugged at the horrible plant, but its vines were the size of thick ropes and bore large leaves that kept getting in the way. Its black-tipped tendrils coiled tightly around their hands and fingers, preventing them from casting any kind of spell, and its blossoms of orange, purple, and yellow moved from side to side as if they could hear and see everything that was going on around them.

Albert watched in horror as the vines tightened their stranglehold and tethered the three witches to the ends of the stacks.

Bianca looked up at Albert and managed to blurt out, "Cobras Carnivisauthrius!" before being gagged by the corner of a massive leaf. Then Albert heard a soft clinking noise, as the vial containing the blue-green liquid that was Prudence's antidote slipped from Bianca's hand and rolled across the floor.

As frightened as Albert was, he knew what he had to do. No matter what the risk, he had to make his way to the thimble-size pot and pluck a leaf small enough for him to carry back to Ailie for positive identification. Albert mustered all the courage he could find and set off on his mission, all too aware that the fate of his beloved friends rested solely in his paws.

With no regard for his own safety, Albert climbed upward through the venting system and into the adult library. He then proceeded down the long hall that housed the administration offices, squeezed under the director's door, and went straight to the tiny clay pot that sat under the grow light in the corner of the office. Quickly, he jerked a small leaf from near the base of the plant. The plant appeared to wince then began to shake as if in a rage.

Albert wasted no time making his escape. More determined than ever to get the leaf back to Ailie, he made a heroic jump from the window ledge to a first-floor gutter and scurried down the drainpipe that led to the street below. A rustling noise from behind alerted him that one of the plant's sinister vines was in close pursuit. Clutching the leaf securely in his jaws, Albert took off down the street without daring so much as a glance backward. Therefore, he did not see the menacing, black-tipped tendrils produce small, white fangs that struck out at him barely missing their mark. Nor did he hear the low, hissing noise the plant made before coming to an abrupt halt and recoiling back into the brick building.

25

Snake Charmer's Plant

Eve and Paisley were just waking up from their naps when Albert came flying through the greenhouse door as though his tail was on fire, and scaled the leg of Bianca's mahogany desk so quickly one would have thought him part squirrel.

The two cats jumped onto the desk after their friend and watched as the small mouse struggled to regain his breath.

"Albert, what on earth happened?" questioned a concerned Ailie.

Emily grabbed a yellow Post-it note from the side of the desk and began fanning her brother, who sat gulping air into his winded lungs.

Once Albert had managed to catch his breath, he recounted the events that had unfolded in the library. When he got to the part where the vines attacked the witches, Eve and Paisley leaped from the desk and sprang toward the door.

"Where are you going?" yelled Bailey after them.

"To our witches, of course," came the reply.

"No! Wait!" yelled Bailey. "It could be dangerous!" But by then the cats were out the door and gone.

"You could not have stopped them," said Ailie, patting Bailey on the hand. "There's no end to the depths of devotion a cat feels for her witch." She then turned to Albert. "Were you able to secure a piece of that plant?"

"Yes," said Albert, handing over the leaf. "Oh, and I almost forgot to tell you, Bianca was able to blurt out 'Cobras Carnivisauthrius' before being gagged."

"Cobras Carnivisauthrius!" exclaimed Ailie, examining the leaf. All the color drained from the Scottish mouse's whiskers. "This cannot be," said Ailie, turning the leaf over in her paws. "I mean, it is, but it can't be." She began pacing from one end of the desk to the other. "Cobras Carnivisauthrius," explained Ailie, "is a very rare snake charmer's plant. The plant actually falls under its handler's spell and does his bidding. Unfortunately, only people with evil intentions can handle the plant, but it's been extinct for over a hundred years. At least, everyone thought it was." She ran to one of the books that lay open on the desk and turned its pages until she came to a series of pictures of the plant that Albert had just seen in the library. The photographs chronicled the plant's growth from the time it sprouted from a small pot until it was fully grown. The last picture showed a mature plant, baring fangs and striking at the camera.

"If the townspeople have been inhaling particles of a Cobras Carnivisauthrius, it's no wonder their tempers are flaring," said Ailie. "That plant is evil through and through."

"Well, how do we get rid of this Cobras Carnivisauthrius?" asked Bailey.

"That's the problem," cried Ailie. "I'm not certain we can. The only way to get rid of a Cobras Carnivisauthrius is with a night-blooming Mongoosias Muscipulanthrius." She turned the page and pointed to a picture of a benevolent-looking plant with a thin stem and a delicate, white flower. "The problem is I don't know where to find a night-blooming Mongoosias Muscipulanthrius. They're extremely rare. I'm not even sure one still exists."

"Oh, one still exists," said Albert, staring at the plant in the book, "and I know where it is."

For the second time that day all eyes were on Albert, who now had to explain just how it was that he knew where to find a rare, night-blooming Mongoosias Muscipulanthrius.

"Bailey, do you remember when we were at Witchfest and I got lost—err, I mean, went exploring in the caverns?" The correction had been made solely for Ailie's benefit.

"Yes," said Bailey, looking intently at Albert.

"Well, remember when you found me relaxing in that cavern? Directly across from me, clinging to the rock on the side of the wall, was a Mongoosias Muscipulanthrius."

"Albert, are you sure it was a Mongoosias Muscipulanthrius?" asked Bailey.

"Yes," said Albert. "I mean, as certain as a mouse can be."

"Well, we have got to get to that plant," stated Ailie. "And once we get to it, we have to handle it properly." She ran into her cottage and returned carrying a mouse-size book. "Everything we need to know about handling the Mongoosias Muscipulanthrius is in this book," she said. She opened to the section on rare, night-blooming plants and began scouring the page with her paw. "Yes, here it is. Let me see. It says here that the night-blooming Mongoosias Muscipulanthrius is the only plant that has the ability to destroy a Cobras Carnivisauthrius. It does this by doing battle with the plant." She closed the book and looked up at Bailey. "We have to get to the Caverns of Hanhoo and retrieve that plant, and we have to do it now. Time may be running out. The larger that Cobras Carnivisauthrius gets, the more dangerous it becomes."

Bailey looked down at the small mouse staring anxiously up at her from the desk.

"Bailey, dear," said Ailie. "All the witches in town are out helping to keep the townspeople from fighting with one another. We don't have time to track anyone down. If we're going to save our friends and this town, we're going to have to do it now. Do you have any suggestions?"

Bailey bit down nervously on her bottom lip. "Yes, well, maybe," she said, going over to the bookshelf and retrieving a spell book. "There should be a transportation spell in here somewhere. Yes, here it is. This should get us to the Caverns of Hanhoo. That is if I can get it to work. Transportation spells are very tricky. I should warn you that if I don't cast it correctly, we could end up any number of places, but I'm willing to try if you are."

"I have total faith in your abilities as a witch," said Ailie.

"How are we going to find the Mongoosias Muscipulanthrius once we get there?" asked Albert, who was beginning to feel a little more than uncomfortable about the prospect of their upcoming adventure. "Those tunnels are very complicated. It could take us hours to find our way back to that particular cavern."

"Just leave that to me," said Bailey. "Now, let me see how this spell works." She studied the page for a few minutes then looked at the others. "I think I've got it," she said, sounding a little unsure of herself. "At least, I hope I do." She lowered her hand, and Albert and Ailie climbed on, followed closely by Emily.

"Emily, no, you can't go," said Albert sternly to his little sister. "It's too dangerous."

"I'm going, and you can't stop me," said Emily, stomping, her foot.

"Emily, we need you here," said Ailie. "I've put a call in to the Wexford Institute asking that they have Hildegard Harrowitz come and help us with this problem. If she shows up while we're away, we're counting on you to tell her where to find us. It's a very imporrrtant job. Do you think you can do this for us, Emily?"

"Of course," said Emily, who was a bit embarrassed by her earlier foot stomping. "I'll do whatever you need."

"Well, then, are we ready?" asked Bailey.

"Wait," said Ailie, looking down at her book. "We'll need a pot to carry the Mongoosias Muscipulanthrius in. Bailey, could you grab one of those six-inch clay pots from the work bench?"

Bailey placed Albert and Ailie carefully on her shoulder and retrieved the pot from the bench. "Ready?" she asked again.

"As ready as we'll ever be," said Albert.

Bailey tucked the pot between her ankles and placed her arms out in front of her. She then began to cast the spell she had found in the book.

"Song of a storm," she said. And a wind began to rustle inside the greenhouse.

"Drawing of light." And a flash of lightning pierced the room.

"Spreading my wings," she continued, stretching her arms to her sides.

"I now shall take flight!" With these final words came a loud clap of thunder, and the three disappeared from sight.

"I hope they arrive safely," said Emily meekly after they had vanished. Then she sat down on the edge of the desk and pulled wearily at her whiskers.

26

Back to the Caverns of Hanhoo

The next thing Albert knew, he and Ailie were
sitting on Bailey's shoulder in a rather dark, damp tunnel
in the Caverns of Hanhoo.

"We made it," said Bailey, reaching between her
ankles to retrieve the clay pot. "Now all we have to do is
find the Mongoosias Muscipulanthrius." She reached into
her pocket, pulled out the directional ring she had been
given at Witchfest, and placed it carefully on her right
index finger. "To the Mongoosias Muscipulanthrius," she
said to the ring. The silver compass point inside the ring
face spun around several times, then pointed directly in
front of them. The group followed the tunnel straight
ahead until they reached a cross section, and the arrow's
sharp point spun to the left. They followed as directed and
were suddenly met by the strong smell of rotten fish.

"Oh, my," said Ailie, pinching her nose closed.
"What is that awful smell?"

"I'm afraid it's Irwin's stuffed fish," said Bailey nervously.

"Who's Irwin?" questioned Ailie.

"He's a rather disagreeable genie that lives here in the caverns," answered Bailey, looking cautiously around her.

Ailie lowered her voice and said, "We'll need to be very careful. Genies are not to be dealt with lightly. There was this one named Kazmar—"

"I know all about Kazmar," interrupted Bailey, lowering her voice to a whisper. She did not mean to be rude, but the last thing she needed was to be reminded of the evil genie. Her stomach was tied up in knots as it was. "I can see Irwin's fish hanging on the wall up ahead. If we're very quiet perhaps he won't hear us."

Albert and Ailie sat quiet as church mice on Bailey's shoulder as she tiptoed past Irwin. They had just made it past the fish and were almost home free when they heard a loud rumble and turned to see smoke billowing from the fish's mouth.

"Why have you disturbed my slumber?" thundered the genie's deep voice.

"We were just passing through. Now, if you'll excuse us, we'll be on our way," said Bailey sternly.

"I think not!" roared the genie.

"Watch yourself, or you'll suffer the same fate as Kazmar," said Bailey, repeating the words she had heard the High Witch use to put the genie in his place.

"And who's going to rob me of my powers, the likes of you?" roared the genie. "Why, you don't even have a cat!"

"No, but I do," came a voice from directly in front of the genie. The group watched as Hildegard Harrowitz and Charm materialized in front of their eyes.

"No harm meant, really, Hildegard," said Irwin. "Just trying to frighten them a little is all."

A wave of relief swept over Bailey as she saw the genie begin to cower.

"Hildegard, how did you find us?" asked Bailey.

"I got Ailie's message and went by the greenhouse. Emily told me you were here. What she didn't tell me was *how* you got here."

"I found a transportation spell in one of Bianca's books," said Bailey.

"You cast a transportation spell all by yourself, and it worked?" said Hildegard, staring at Bailey.

"Yes, ma'am," answered the young witch.

Charm, who had been sitting at Hildegard's feet, walked over to Bailey and brushed up against her legs.

"That's quite an accomplishment," said Hildegard, "even Charm's impressed. But Bailey, how did you plan on finding the plant once you got here?"

"I still have my ring from Witchfest," said Bailey, holding her hand out so Hildegard could see. "I figured the Mongoosias Muscipulanthrius must have been here and in place when the directional spell was cast on the caverns, so it would point me in the right direction, and so far, so good."

"Clever girl," said Hildegard, raising an eyebrow. "You all run ahead and find that plant, then meet me back here. Irwin and I need to have a little chat."

Hildegard gave Irwin a dirty look. The genie swallowed hard and began to tremble.

Bailey placed a protective hand over Albert and Ailie, then hurried off down the tunnel, stopping occasionally to check her ring. It wasn't long before the compass point once again turned to the left, directing the group to the opening of one of the caverns. There, clinging to the wall as if for dear life, just as Albert had remembered, was the rare, night-blooming Mongoosias Muscipulanthrius.

Bailey went directly over to the plant and tugged gently at the part of its stem closest to the roots, but the plant dug in and held on.

"You can't just pull at it like that," scolded Ailie from Bailey's shoulder. "The Mongoosias Muscipulanthrius is a very sensitive plant. You have to ask it politely. And according to the book, it helps to have someone it's been in contact with before do the asking. Albert that would be you."

"What do I do?" asked Albert.

"Well, it's best if you explain the problem to the plant and then ask it to help. Oh, yes, one other thing. By the shape of its leaves, I would venture to say it's a lady plant, so you may want to address her as 'Miss.'"

Albert felt a little silly talking to a plant, but he remembered telling his father what now seemed like ages ago that *a mouse has got to do what a mouse has got to do'*, so he cleared his throat, stood up tall, and bowed from the waist.

"Miss Mongoosias," he began, "we seem to be having trouble with a Cobras Carnivisauthrius. Would you please do us the great favor of accompanying us back to the Harborville Library and ridding us of this nuisance by doing battle with the dreadful thing?"

"Well done," said Ailie.

Bailey held out the clay pot they had brought, and to everyone's relief, the Mongoosias Muscipulanthrius loosened its stranglehold on the cavern's rock wall and crept into the container, where it stood with its petals closed up tight. It then leaned its delicate white bud forward and nudged Albert gently on his shoulder.

"You know, Albert," said Bailey teasingly, "I think she likes you."

"Nice plant," said Albert, petting the top of the plant's petals.

The group retraced their steps back to where they had left Hildegard. When they arrived, they found that the gaping mouth of Irwin's fish had been sewn shut.

"Hildegard, surely we can talk this over reasonably," came a muffled voice from inside the fish.

"Why have you sewn Irwin up in his fish?" asked Bailey, who was a bit relieved that the genie was not on the loose.

"Because," said Hildegard, "Irwin has been a very bad genie. It turns out that fish he calls home had swallowed the map showing the burial location of Kazmar's lamp. Irwin knows that if Kazmar gets his hands on his lost lamp, he will have the power to do whatever he pleases. So Irwin made a deal with him. Irwin would hand over the map if Kazmar would give him full control of the caverns."

"You mean to tell me—" began Albert.

"That's right," finished Hildegard. "The town of Harborville built its library directly over Kazmar's lamp."

"So it was Kazmar that Albert saw in the basement with Miss Prattle?" asked Bailey.

"I'm afraid so," answered Hildegard. "He's poisoned Prudence and has her doing his bidding. That's why she has been grinding up the Cobras Carnivisauthrius and blowing it out into the wind for the townspeople to inhale."

"But why?" asked Albert.

"Because," said Hildegard, "Kazmar knew once the townspeople inhaled particles of that evil plant they would be far too busy fighting with one another to notice any odd digging that might be going on in or around the library. He didn't want anyone interfering with his search for his lamp, and his plan worked perfectly. No one in Harborville has noticed anything odd at all. They've been far too busy trying to make their neighbors as miserable as they are."

"It makes sense," said Ailie. "He must be the one handling the plant. I knew it couldn't be Prudence. She's too good a witch to handle that evil thing. It would never respond to her. It's only the poison making her behave the way she is."

"We're going to have to get to the library and stop Kazmar from getting back into his lamp," said Hildegard. "If he reunites with his powers there's no end to the trouble he'll cause. Hope everyone's ready for this," and she gave an elaborate sweep of her arm.

27

Kazmar's Lamp and a Mouse Extraordinaire

Albert heard the sound of wind rush by his ears, and he felt an odd, swirling motion. For a brief moment everything went fuzzy. When his vision cleared, he and Ailie were standing on the floor next to Bailey in the basement of the library.

He shook his head and focused on the scene before him. Standing waist deep in a hole was a very thin man who was clawing at the ground with a pickax. Next to him, digging with a shovel, was Miss Prattle. Albert would not have believed it possible, but the director's features had become even sharper and her skin had taken on a sickly green tinge.

"Looking for something, Kazmar?" glowered Hildegard, who had positioned herself at the edge of the hole in front of the genie.

"Found is more like it," sneered the evil genie as his ax struck metal.

"Drop the ax and come out of there," said Hildegard sternly to the genie. She raised her hands in front of her and prepared to cast a spell. Bailey moved bravely to Hildegard's side. Charm stood between the two witches and glared at Kazmar, her sapphire blue eyes all but shooting sparks.

"Don't even think about it," sneered Kazmar, a sinister smile beginning to form on his face. "Unless you want your friends upstairs to be crushed! One word from me and my plant will tighten its grip."

Albert could hear a scraping sound coming from the ceiling above them as Kazmar's evil plant dragged itself across the floor. He thought of his friends upstairs with the snaking vines of the Cobras Carnivisauthrius coiled about them and knew they had to act quickly.

"Ailie, use the Mongoosias Muscipulanthrius," whispered Albert.

"Our plant can't do battle with his plant until the moon comes out and she blooms," whispered back Ailie through clenched teeth.

They all watched as Kazmar reached into the earth and pulled a tarnished silver lamp from the dirt.

"Albert, we have to stop Kazmar from getting into that lamp!" cried Ailie in a panicked whisper.

"Help Hildegard keep Kazmar busy. I'll be right back," said Albert, and he took off in the direction of the stairway.

Albert raced up the stairs as fast as his legs would carry him. When he got to the top he ran to the children's corner, plunged his paw into the hem of the bright-blue curtains, felt around until he found the shrinking spectacles Cat had given him, and placed them securely on his nose.

He looked over to where Catrina, Annie, and Bianca stood tethered to the ends of the stacks. Eve and Paisley were circling the shelves, hissing and clawing at the nasty vine in an attempt to keep it from sinking its fangs into the witches. "I'll be back," he promised under his breath and raced back down the stairs.

Albert returned to the basement just as Prudence and Kazmar were climbing out of the hole they had dug.

Kazmar brushed the dirt from his lamp. "Hold this," demanded the genie, as he handed the lamp to Prudence.

Albert watched as Prudence took the lamp from Kazmar's hands and held it out in front of her.

The genie then threw back his head, gave a horrible laugh, dissolved into ghastly gray smoke, and prepared to enter his lamp.

Trying desperately to clear his mind of the events unfolding around him, Albert concentrated as hard as he could and stared at the lamp through his shrinking glasses. *I hope you work on more than books*, he thought to himself.

The gray smoke that was the genie began to circle the lamp preparing to make its entrance through the long silver spout, but just as Kazmar was about to squeeze through the narrow opening, the lamp began to quiver. It then began to shake violently, and before either the genie or Prudence knew what was happening, it shrank to less than a quarter of an inch and slipped through Prudence's fingers.

Making a mad dash forward, Albert intercepted the slip of silver that had fallen from Prudence's fumbling hands. He threaded his tail through the lamp's loopy handle, and dragging the small, silver lamp behind him, darted toward the tunnels the witches had conjured.

"Tell Hildegard to meet me for coffee," Albert yelled over his shoulder. Then he disappeared through the portal marked with a house for Merris Merriweather's real estate office.

Kazmar gave a loud, anguished howl and flew off after Albert. Albert, who knew the tunnels like the back of his paw, led the genie deeper and deeper into the maze that made up the transit system. In his smoky state, Kazmar had no trouble navigating the twists and turns that made up the maze, but as limber as the genie was, he was still no match for Albert, who had the home tunnel advantage. Albert would fake left, then turn right to confuse the genie. The trick, he told himself, was to make sure he had just the right amount of distance between himself and Kazmar when they exited the tunnels through the library portal marked with a cup and saucer for the Earthly Brew Coffee House. He hoped that Bailey had picked up on his clue about meeting for coffee and that Hildegard would have a plan to deal with the genie when he exited the tunnel back into the library's basement. If not, well…Albert didn't want to think about that.

The small mouse ran until his legs began to feel like rubber, then circling back, he found the proper portal exit, drew upon all his strength, and sprinted out, leaving the genie a few seconds behind.

Hildegard stood ready and waiting in the library's basement. As soon as she saw Albert safely exit the tunnel, she slapped a mason jar she had found in the corner of the room over the portal and watched as gray smoke filled the glass. Quickly, she removed the jar, slapped its lid in place, and screwed it down tightly, making certain the seal was secure. She then raised the jar and stared through the glass. Two angry eyeballs stared back out at her from amid the gray smoke she had managed to imprison.

"Oh, Alberrrrrt," gasped Ailie, as she threw her arms around a winded Albert, "that was the brrravest thing I've ever seen!"

"Albert, you're a genius," said Hildegard, giving the jar a good shake. "Now hold on, because we have to get upstairs in a hurry." The High Witch gave an elaborate sweep of her arm, and the entire group found themselves on the first floor.

Charm immediately went to the aid of Eve and Paisley, who were bravely hissing and clawing at the Cobras Carnivisauthrius.

Hildegard quickly placed the pot with the Mongoosias Muscipulanthrius directly in front of the window.

A white saucer moon was just beginning to rise in the August night sky, and it was only a matter of seconds before the first moonbeams found their way to the window. The moment the soft light spilled through onto the Mongoosias Muscipulanthrius, the plant lifted its porcelain-white bud toward the moon and bloomed. The plant opened its delicate, white petals to expose a fierce looking mouth with sharp teeth, and its thin stem lengthened, allowing it to twist, turn, and weave.

The Cobras Carnivisauthrius immediately turned its attention from the witches to its adversary. Snaking and coiling, it hissed and struck out at the small, white petals of the Mongoosias Muscipulanthrius. But try as it might, it could not touch the thin-stemmed plant that dodged, wove, and slapped at the larger plant with her small, white petals.

The plants began circling each other, watching for an opportunity to attack. Then suddenly, with no warning, the Mongoosias Muscipulanthrius pounced. Grabbing the tip of one of the evil plant's grotesque leaves in its mouth, it closed its petals tightly around the leaf. The Cobras Carnivisauthrius tried with all its might to pull away from the Mongoosias Muscipulanthrius, but its efforts were in vain. Albert watched in amazement as their plant bore down hard on Kazmar's plant and began to swallow, inhaling its opponent very much the way a child slurps down a spaghetti noodle. Soon Kazmar's evil plant completely disappeared into the thin stem of the Mongoosias Muscipulanthrius. The thin-stemmed plant then lifted its tightly closed petals toward the ceiling and gave a small belch that sent the thimble-size pot Kazmar's plant had been rooted in sailing to the floor. It then shook its delicate, white petals and retreated to its clay pot.

"Are you three all right?" asked Hildegard of the witches who were now free of the plant.

"I'm fine. How about you two?" asked Cat.

"I'm fine," said Annie. "Bianca, are you all right?"

"Yes," answered Bianca. "Thank goodness Eve and Paisley showed up when they did. Remind me to start seriously looking for a proper cat." She then walked over and picked up the vial of blue-green liquid she had been forced to drop earlier. "Good, it didn't break," she said, examining the vial. "We need to get this potion into Prudence."

Everyone turned their attention to Prudence, who stood glaring out at them from the children's corner.

"Prudence," said Cat kindly, looking at the poisoned witch with her sharp features and sickly, green skin, "you're very ill, and you need to drink this potion in order to get well."

Prudence narrowed her beady eyes and stared back at Cat with a mean look. "Stay away from me," she hissed.

"Come on, Prudence," said Annie, calmly walking toward the witch, "be a good witch and take your medicine."

But Prudence began to stomp her feet and flail her arms so that no one could get near her.

The Mongoosias Muscipulanthrius, which had been sitting quietly by, slowly started to stretch its long, thin stem toward Prudence. Tenderly, it coiled itself around the sick witch and plunked her down on the soft seat of the rocking chair.

"Thank you," said Bianca to the plant. "This should make matters easier." She walked over to Prudence and held the vial to her mouth, but Prudence pressed her lips together and refused to open them. Bianca pinched Prudence's nose closed, thinking she would have to open her mouth to breathe, but Prudence just parted her lips into a nasty sneer and hissed in air through her gritted teeth.

"Well, I don't know what to do," said Bianca. "I can't get this down her if she won't open her mouth."

Ailie, who had crawled up the side of the rocking chair and was sitting on the chair's top rung next to Prudence's head, gave the sick witch a determined look.

"Bianca, be ready now," said Ailie, "because in just a minute, Prudence here is going to open her mouth and you must be ready to pour that potion down her throat."

Ailie leaned in and whispered into Prudence's ear, "My dear, I hate to do this to you, but drrrastic times call for drrrastic measures." She then reached up, grabbed a pierced earring that Prudence was wearing in one of her ears, and pulled down and back as hard as she could.

Prudence threw her head back and let out a howl.

Bianca did not miss her opportunity. Quickly, she placed the bottle in Prudence's mouth and poured its contents down her throat, leaving Prudence with no choice but to swallow.

Prudence swallowed, gave a startled yelp, and went limp in the chair.

"Is she all right?" asked Cat, looking worriedly down at the witch who sat slumped over in the rocker.

"She's fine," said Bianca. "Just watch."

In a matter of seconds, Prudence's sharp features began to soften. Her skin lost its sickly, green tint and turned a rosy shade of pink. Then her beady eyes rounded out, and her sharp nose flattened slightly and tilted upward. The scowl the witch wore turned to a sweet smile, and even her hair, which had been cut into a sharp-angled V-shaped pageboy, softened and curled around her face.

"That's the Prudence I know," said Ailie happily from her place on the chair.

"She'll sleep for a few hours," said Bianca, reaching out and pushing the witch's soft curls from her forehead. "Which is good, because the poor thing probably needs the rest."

Albert watched as the Mongoosias Muscipulanthrius carefully unwound itself from the sleeping witch and went to rest back in its container near the window.

"Now all we have to do is get this town back to normal," said Hildegard, as Charm came to stand next to her.

"How do we do that?" asked Albert.

"With a leaf from your friend there," said Bianca, walking over to the plant. She held out her hand, and the Mongoosias Muscipulanthrius delicately dropped one small leaf into her open palm. "All we have to do is grind this up and blow the powder out into the wind."

"Will that be enough?" asked Bailey, looking at the leaf Bianca held in her hand. "It's awfully small."

"Appearances can be deceiving," said Bianca. She placed the leaf in her pocket and, wiggling her fingers in front of her, conjured up a grinder very much like the one Albert had seen in Prudence's office. She then conjured up two large bushel baskets. Bianca dropped the leaf into the end of the grinder and powder began pouring from the other end, enough to fill both baskets.

"Well, it looks like everything here is under control," said Hildegard, smiling happily. "Now, if you'll excuse us, Charm and I need to get Kazmar here to the International Witch's Council, so they can decide his fate." She held up the jar containing the genie.

"Hildegard, wait! You forgot Kazmar's lamp," said Albert, holding up the shrunken piece of metal.

"It's best if we keep Kazmar and his powers parted," said Hildegard. "Albert, I'm leaving the lamp with you. I'm sure you'll come up with some creative way for us witches to keep an eye on it. Take care, everyone," called the High Witch, and she and Charm vanished into thin air.

"Well, what now?" asked Annie.

"To the roof," said Bianca. "We need to blow this powder out into the wind."

Bianca conjured up a cot for Prudence to sleep on and, after tucking the sleeping witch cozily into bed, the group made their way to the roof with the baskets of plant powder.

They were all in such good spirits as they climbed on top of the library's half-shingled roof that they began dancing about in the moonlight. Twirling and swirling, they blew handful after handful of powder out into the warm, night wind and, for the first time in days, a peaceful hush fell over the town of Harborville.

Epilogue
Fond Farewells and Halloween

August ended on a happy note as Harborville got back to normal. The townspeople did not know what had come over them to make them behave so badly, but there were no hard feelings, and everyone was twice as kind as before to make up for things.

The mayor apologized profusely for canceling the Founder's Day festivities and threw the best party the town had ever had. Andrew was given another Good Citizen Award for his self-appointed duties as crossing guard, and the town even purchased a small medal for him. Ellie Goodman was given the honor of placing the medal around the collie's neck, which she did while proclaiming him to be the "bestest, most wonderfulest dog in the whole world."

Albert moved back into his cigar box in the library's basement and watched through the window as autumn came to Harborville, bringing with it a colorful crop of fall leaves, and on the day Prudence left to go back to

Scotland, both he and Ailie were among the friends who showed up at Nature Knows Best to bid her farewell.

"Ailie, are you sure you won't come back with me?" asked Prudence, scooping the small Scottish mouse up in her hand. "The library back home just won't be the same without you."

"No, I think I'll stay here and study American plants for a while," said Ailie. Then she blushed, because everyone knew the real reason she was staying was because she and Albert were sweet on each other. "I do want to apologize one more time for pulling so hard on your earring though," said Ailie. "I know it wasn't nice, but I was desperate."

"Don't be silly," said Prudence. "I don't even remember your pulling my earring. As a matter of fact, I don't remember anything from the time I drank some odd-tasting tea from my thermos in Scotland until I woke up on that cot in the library. Besides, it gave Albert a great idea as to how to keep an eye on Kazmar's powers." She pulled back her hair to expose a small silver earring that looked strikingly like Kazmar's lamp.

Prudence gave Albert a sweet smile, and Albert winked back at her.

"Prudence, are you sure you won't stay for the Halloween celebrations at my barn tonight?" asked Merris Merriweather, who had come to say good-bye. "It's going to be a wonderful party. Hildegard and Charm have even promised to stop by."

"Thank you, but no," said Prudence politely. "I'm afraid I've been away too long as it is. It's very nice of you to include me though, especially after the way I heard I behaved."

"Now, dear, that was not your fault. I just wish we'd known what was going on sooner so you could have been spared becoming so ill," said Merris, dabbing at her eyes with a tissue.

"Bailey, I hope you find just the right cat," said Prudence before leaving. "You're a very special young witch and you deserve the very best."

"Thanks," said Bailey. But the young witch did not hold out much hope. It was All Hallow's Eve, and not one cat had presented itself to her. As a matter of fact, Bailey was beginning to believe that all the kittens in town were avoiding her. She supposed she'd just have to wait another year.

Everyone said their final farewells, then went home to prepare for Merris's party.

It was always a great treat when a witch threw a Halloween party, because a spell was cast around the area so that only witches could enter. This meant that everyone, even the very young, could use magic all night long without upsetting any mortals.

Merris had made certain a tunnel had been conjured so the mice in the area could attend, and Albert and Ailie, who had become a bit of an item, promised to make an appearance.

The party was scheduled to begin at nine that night, and when Bailey arrived at nine thirty, she found Albert and Ailie sitting together on a haystack, nibbling on roasted pumpkin seeds.

"Having fun?" asked Bailey, as large black spiders fell from a twenty-foot-high beam in the center of the barn and landed on some unsuspecting partygoers.

"Oh, it's a terrrrific party," answered Ailie happily.

Bailey laughed as the small children floated catnip-filled balls in the air for Eve, Paisley, and the other cats to leap after. Then she watched as Braden and Sebastian performed their ventriloquist act, which was a bit different in the respect that the boy was the dummy and the cat the ventriloquist.

Just before midnight, everyone gathered in a large circle to sing pumpkin carols, but before the first chord could be struck strange, milky shadows appeared on the barn's high center beam. At first it looked as if the ghosts of two cats had come to join the festivities. Then a hush fell over the barn as it became clear that their guests were Hildegard's Snow Bengal, Charm, accompanied by a small white Bengal kitten.

The kitten looked out over the crowd and locked its sapphire-blue eyes on Bailey. It then turned to its mother and gave a quiet meow as if seeking permission for something. Charm bowed her head to her daughter, and before anyone knew what was happening, the tiny kitten took a daring leap from the high beam straight toward Bailey.

"Oh, my!" yelled Bailey, as she threw out her arms and caught the kitten.

Everyone stood perfectly still as they watched Bailey and the tiny Snow Bengal.

"Well, I would say Bailey trapped that cat securely in her arms, wouldn't you, Annie?" asked Cat, breaking the silence.

"Can't remember having ever seen a more perfect pair," replied Annie.

"Charm's kitten has chosen wisely," proclaimed Hildegard, as she materialized in the center of the room. "Quite wisely, indeed!"

And everyone broke into song as the young witch cradled the soft, white kitten gently in her arms.

Acknowledgements

Thank you to Betsy and Jim. Your help and encouragement through this process has been invaluable.

A special thank you to Bob, for allowing Albert to run freely through his classroom.

Made in the USA
Middletown, DE
30 July 2017